P9-EKD-999

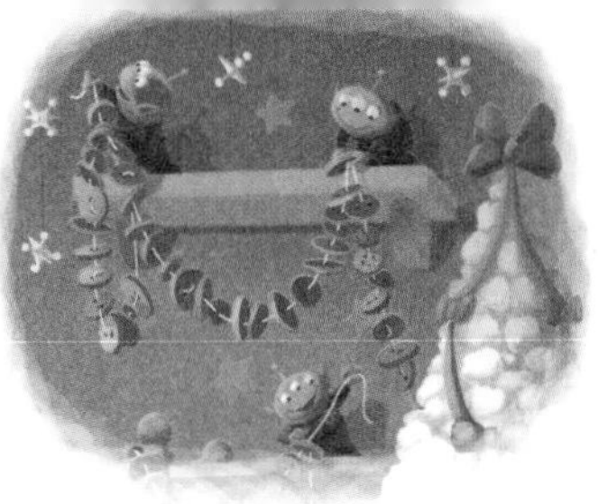

Dear Parent:

Congratulations! Your child is taking the first steps on an exciting journey. The destination? Independent reading!

STEP INTO READING® will help your child get there. The program offers five steps to reading success. Each step includes fun stories and colorful art. There are also Step into Reading Sticker Books, Step into Reading Math Readers, Step into Reading Phonics Readers, Step into Reading Write-In Readers, and Step into Reading Phonics Boxed Sets—a complete literacy program with something to interest every child.

Learning to Read, Step by Step!

Step 1: Ready to Read — Preschool–Kindergarten
• big type and easy words • rhyme and rhythm • picture clues
For children who know the alphabet and are eager to begin reading.

Step 2: Reading with Help — Preschool–Grade 1
• basic vocabulary • short sentences • simple stories
For children who recognize familiar words and sound out new words with help.

Step 3: Reading on Your Own — Grades 1–3
• engaging characters • easy-to-follow plots • popular topics
For children who are ready to read on their own.

Step 4: Reading Paragraphs — Grades 2–3
• challenging vocabulary • short paragraphs • exciting stories
For newly independent readers who read simple sentences with confidence.

Step 5: Ready for Chapters — Grades 2–4
• chapters • longer paragraphs • full-color art
For children who want to take the plunge into chapter books but still like colorful pictures.

STEP INTO READING® is designed to give every child a successful reading experience. The grade levels are only guides. Children can progress through the steps at their own speed, developing confidence in their reading, no matter what their grade.

Remember, a lifetime love of reading starts with a single step!

To the students
of Montclair
Elementary School
—J.L.W.

 Published in the United States by Random House Children's Books, a division of Random House, Inc., 1745 Broadway, New York, NY 10019, and in Canada by Random House of Canada Limited, Toronto, in conjunction with Disney Enterprises, Inc.

Visit us on the Web!
StepIntoReading.com
randomhouse.com/kids

Educators and librarians, for a variety of teaching tools, visit us at randomhouse.com/teachers

ISBN: 978-0-7364-2884-2 (trade) — ISBN: 978-0-7364-8111-3 (lib. bdg.)
Printed in the United States of America 10 9 8 7 6 5 4 3 2 1

STEP INTO READING® STEP 2

Disney · PIXAR TOY STORY

Christmas Toys

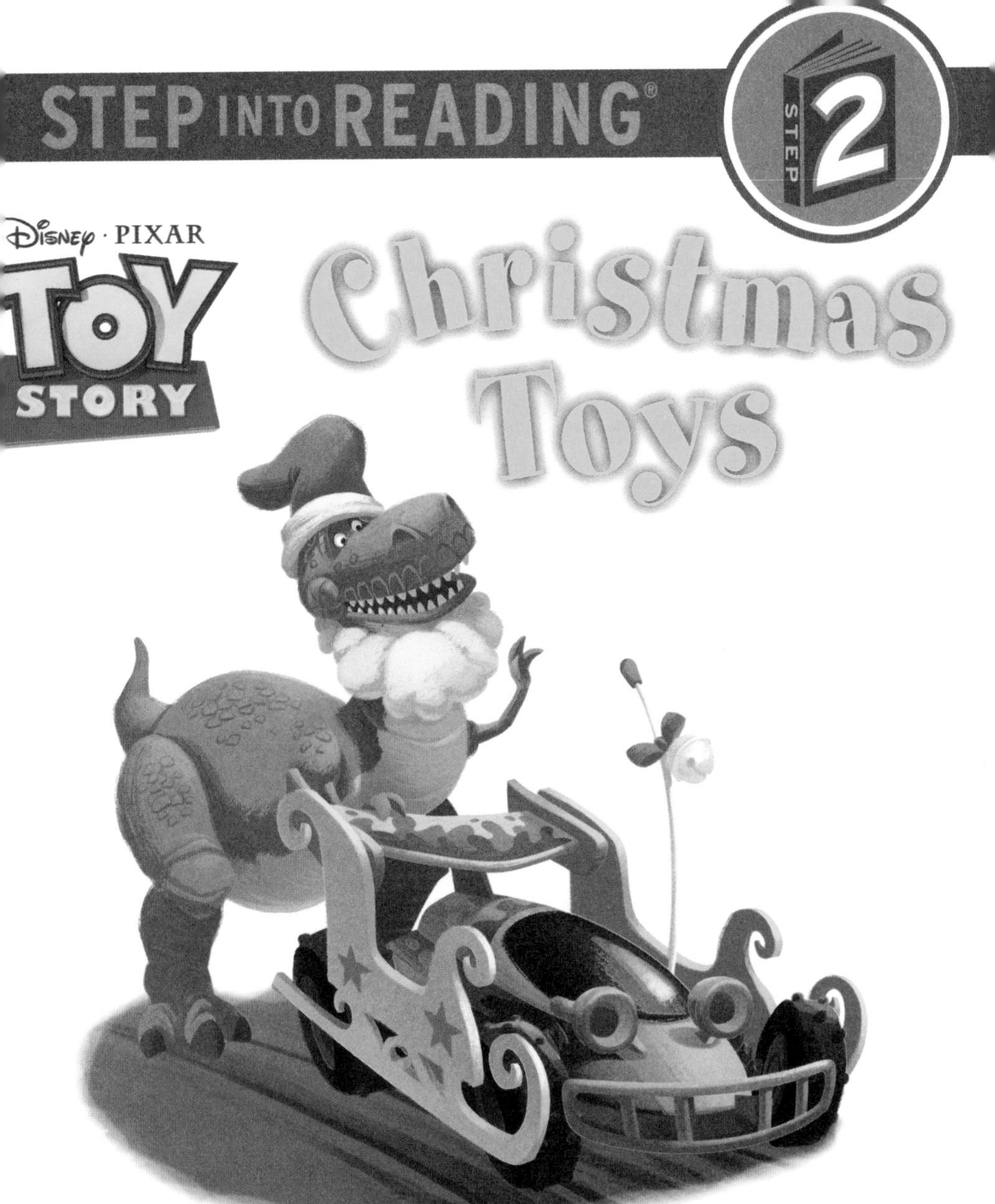

By Jennifer Liberts Weinberg
Illustrated by the Disney Storybook Artists

Random House New York

Andy plays
with Buzz Lightyear
and Sheriff Woody.

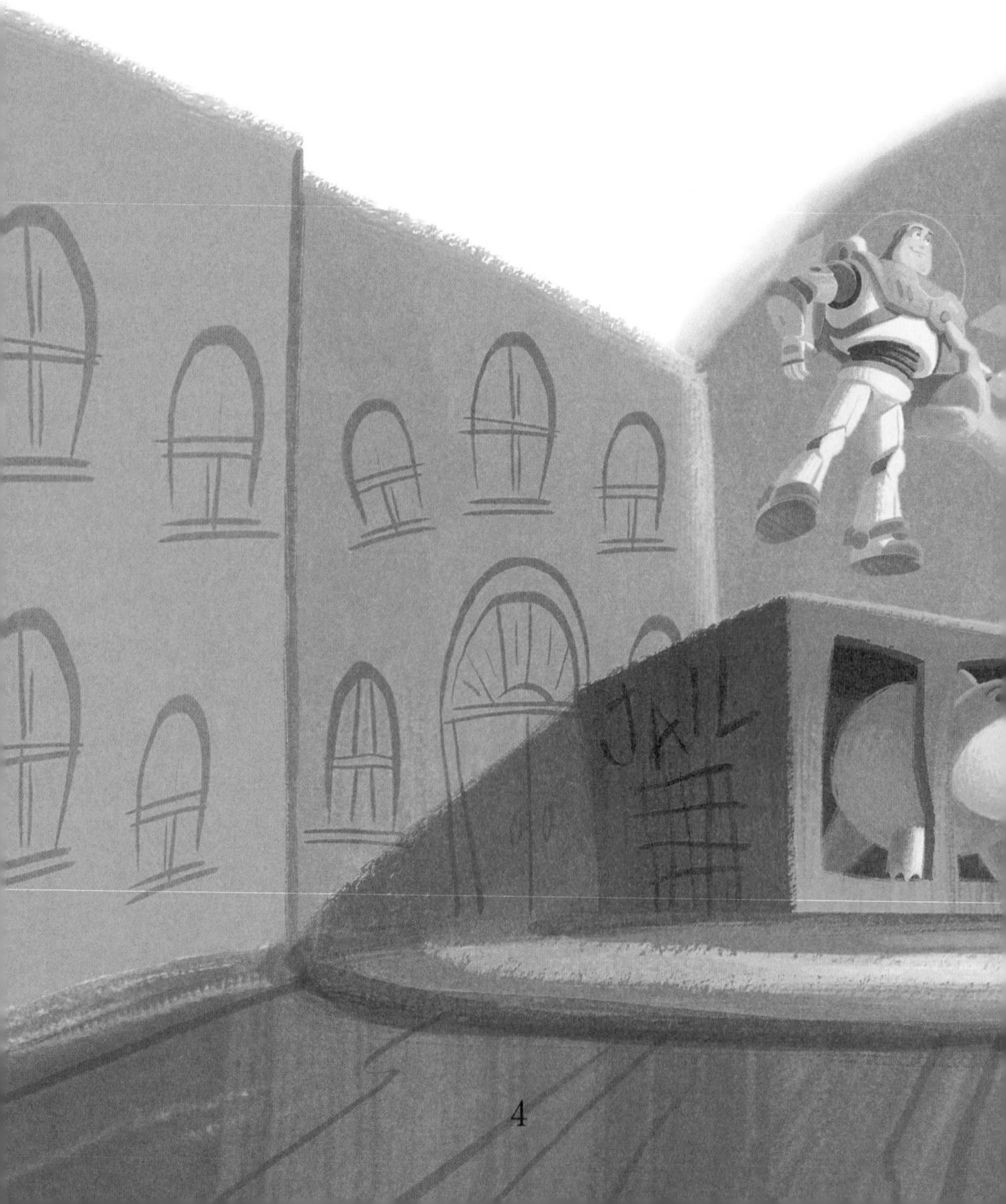
JAIL

They are
his favorite toys.

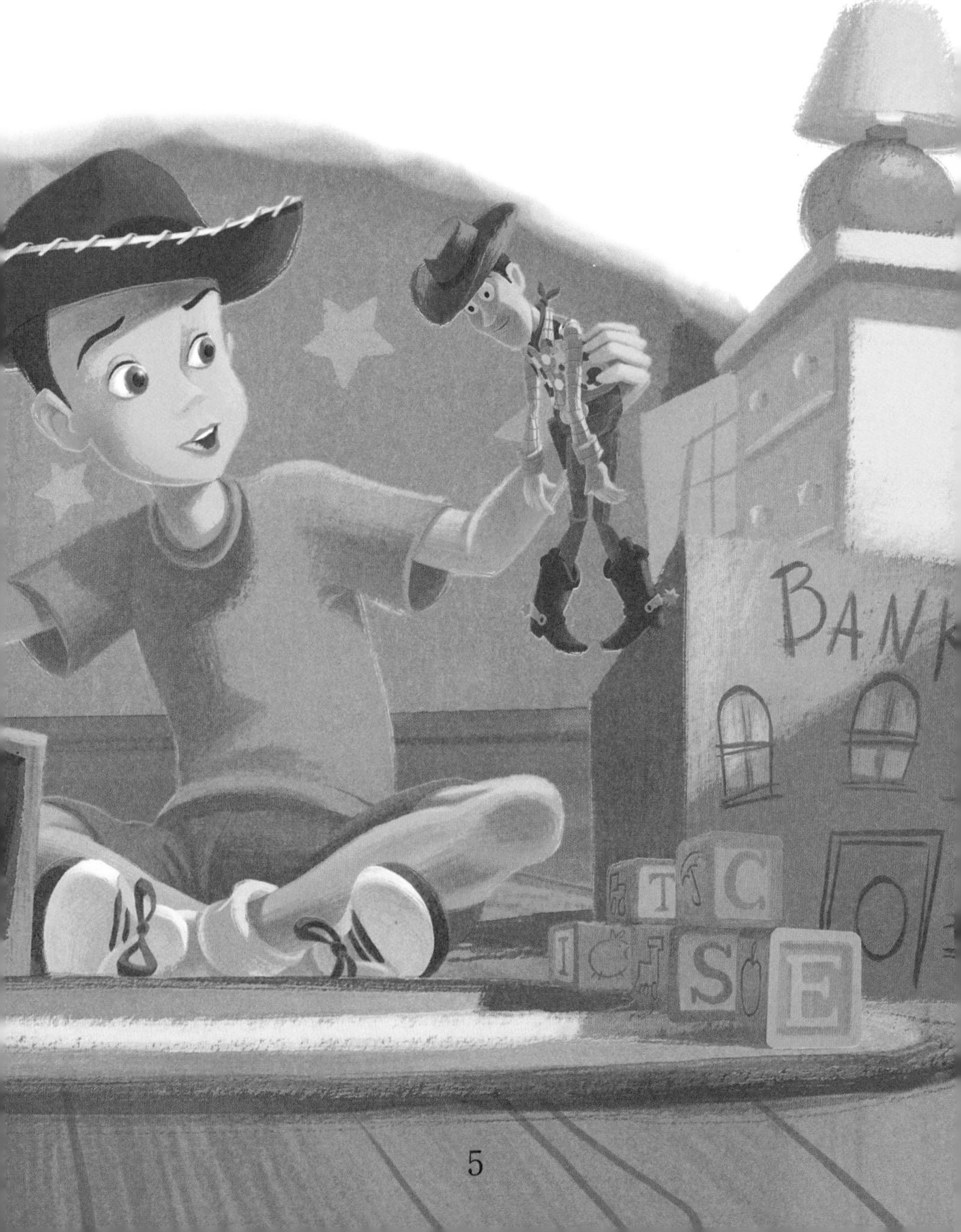
BANK
T
C
I
S
E

Andy's mom
has a surprise.
They are going
on a trip for Christmas!
Andy is happy.
But he cannot
bring his toys.

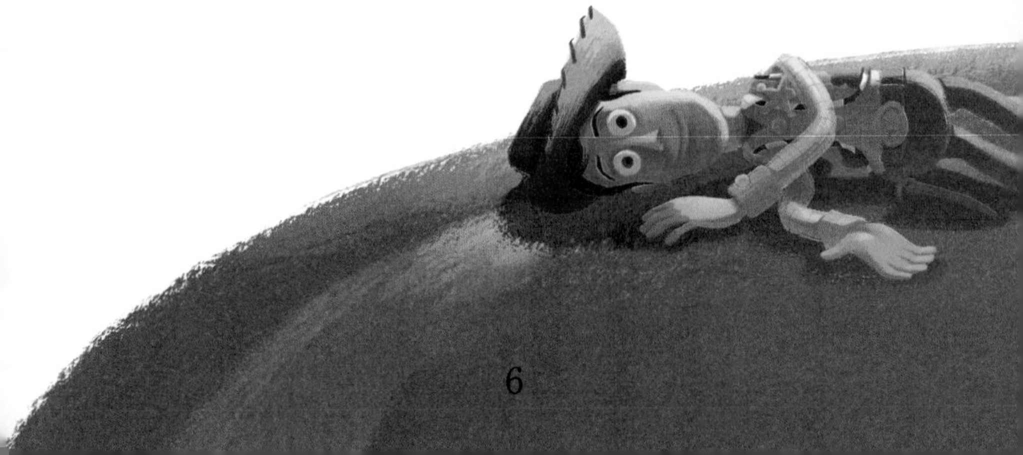

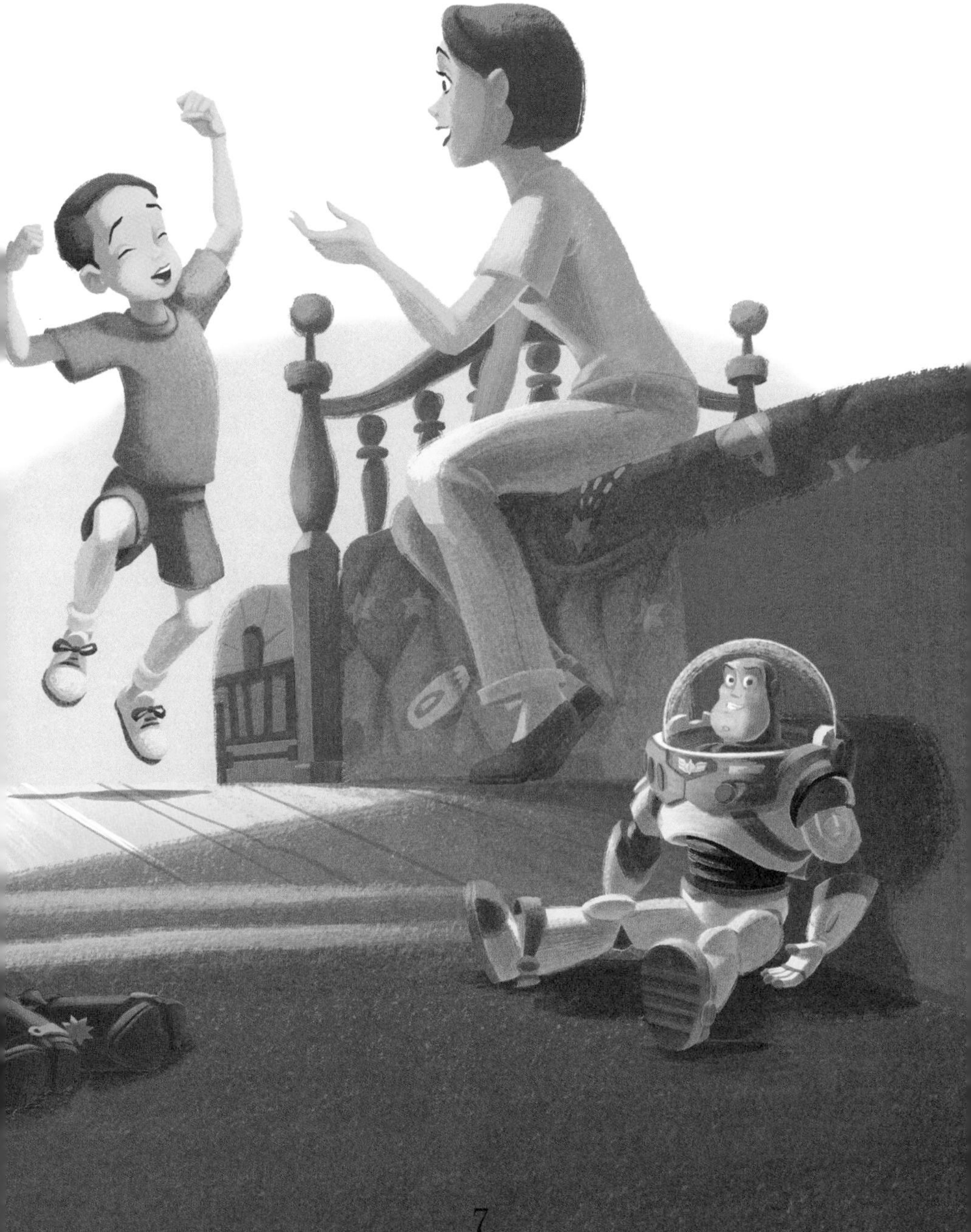

Woody is sad.

He will miss Andy.

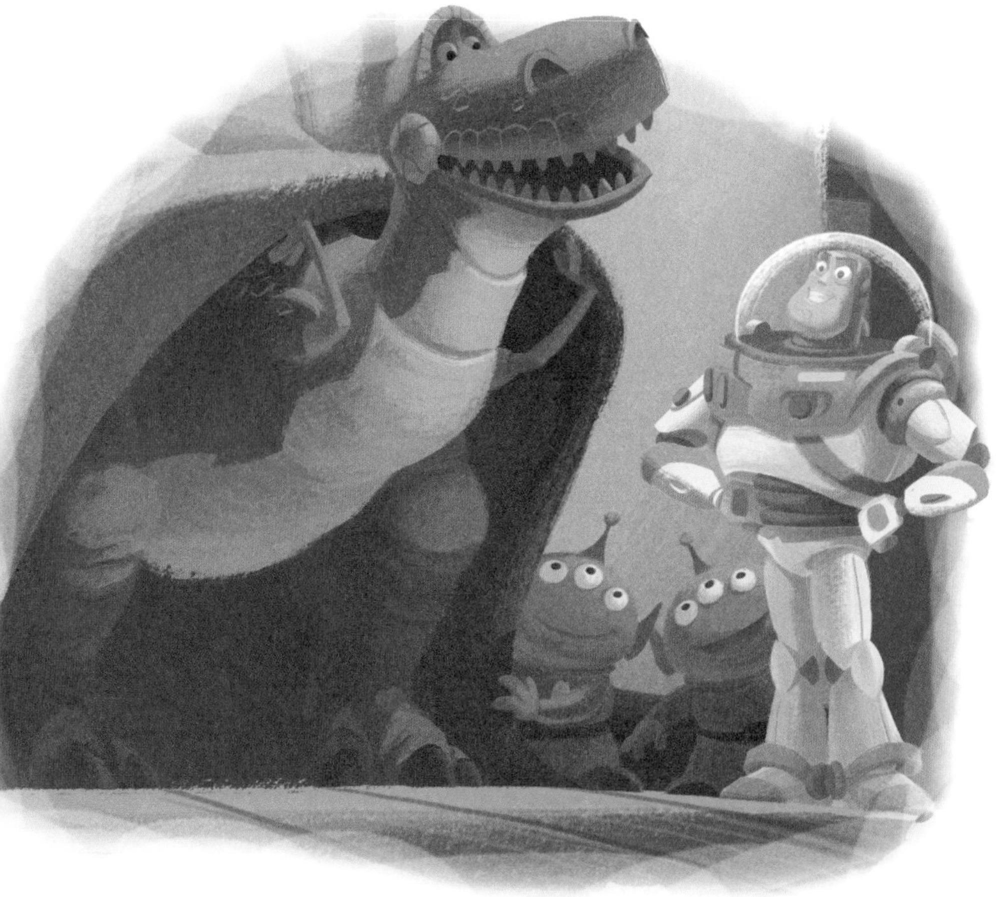

Rex and Buzz want
to cheer Woody up.

Bo Peep and her sheep want to help.

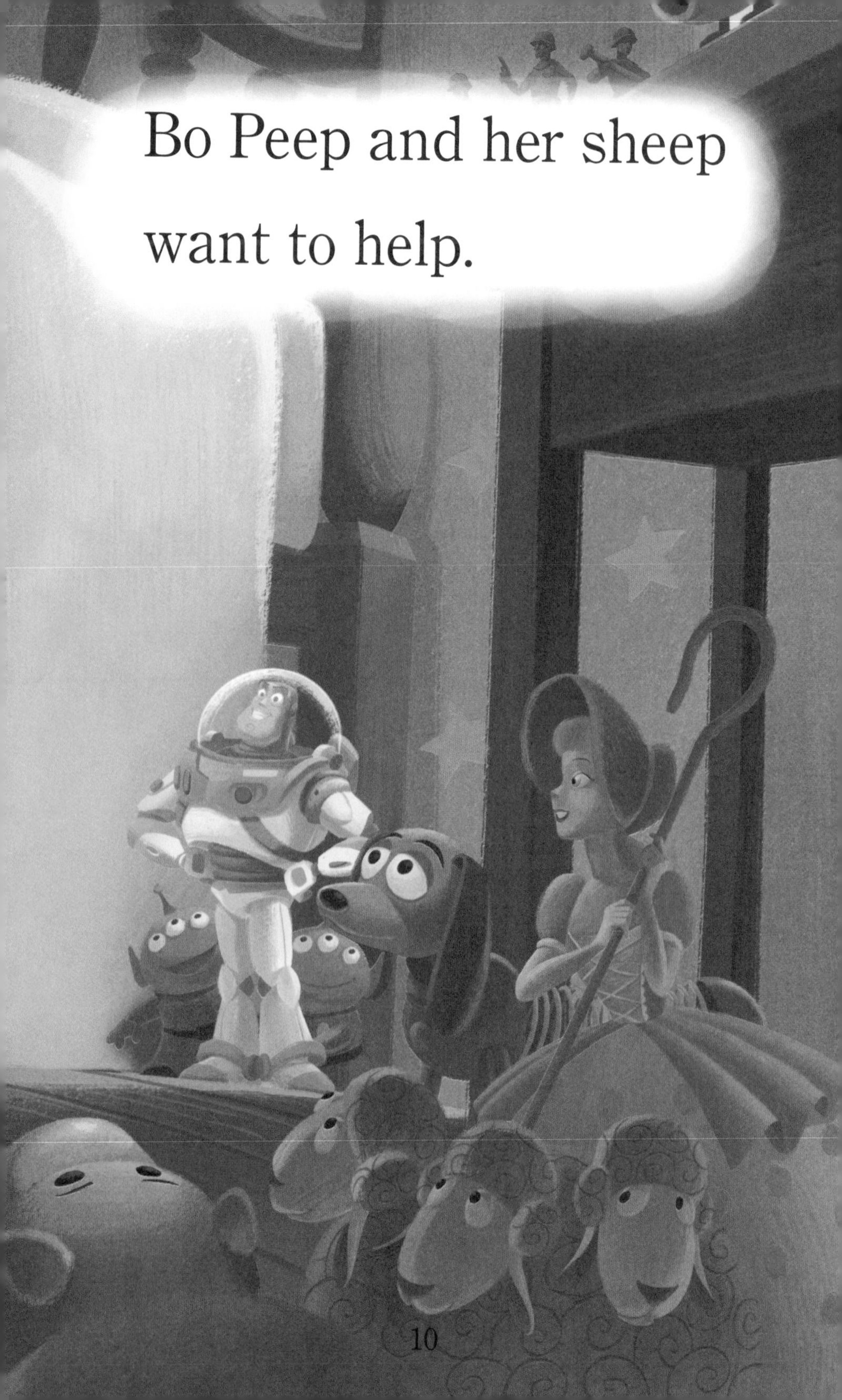

Buzz wants
to give Woody
a toy Christmas!

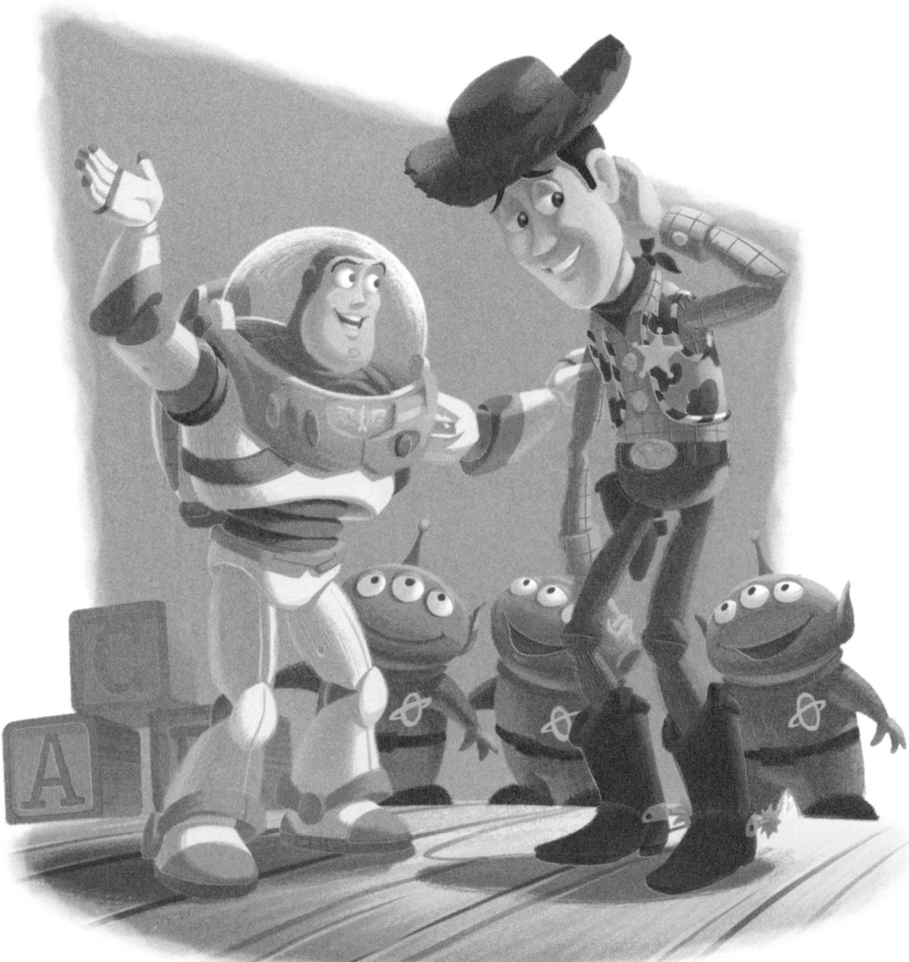

Buzz brings
the toys together.
They make a plan.

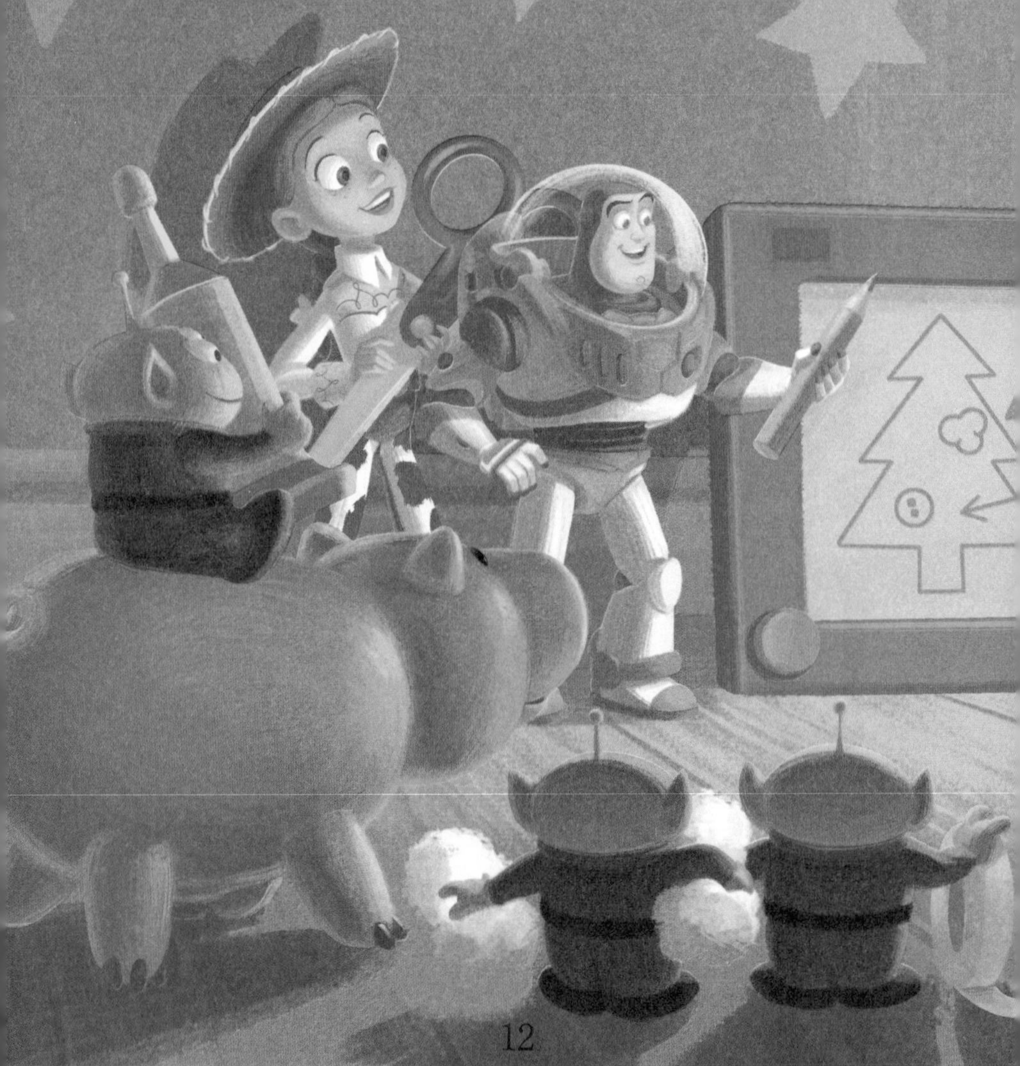

They collect supplies.
They will give Woody
a merry Christmas!

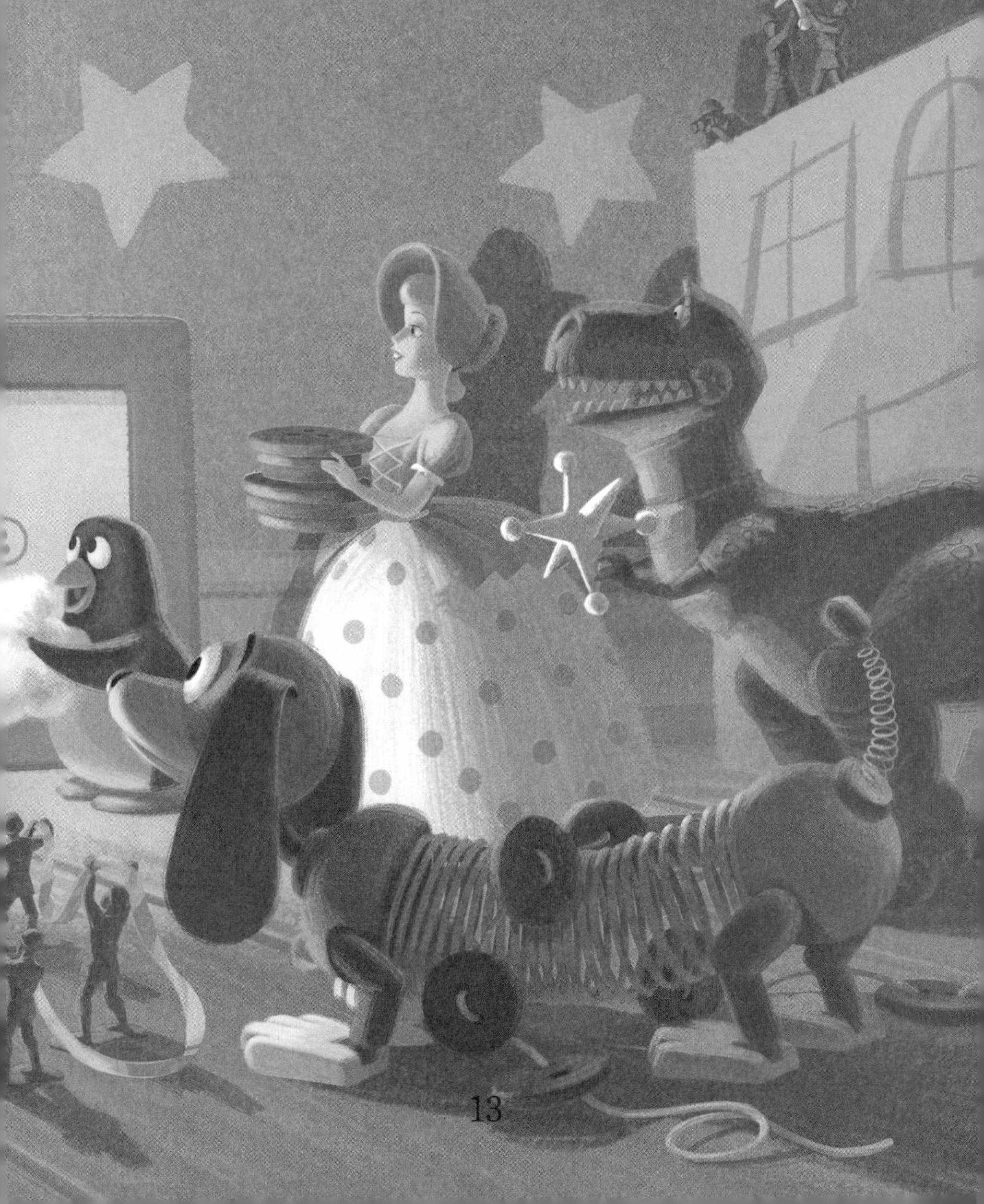

Buzz, Jessie, and Bo Peep
wrap presents.
Rex and Hamm
put the presents
under the tree.

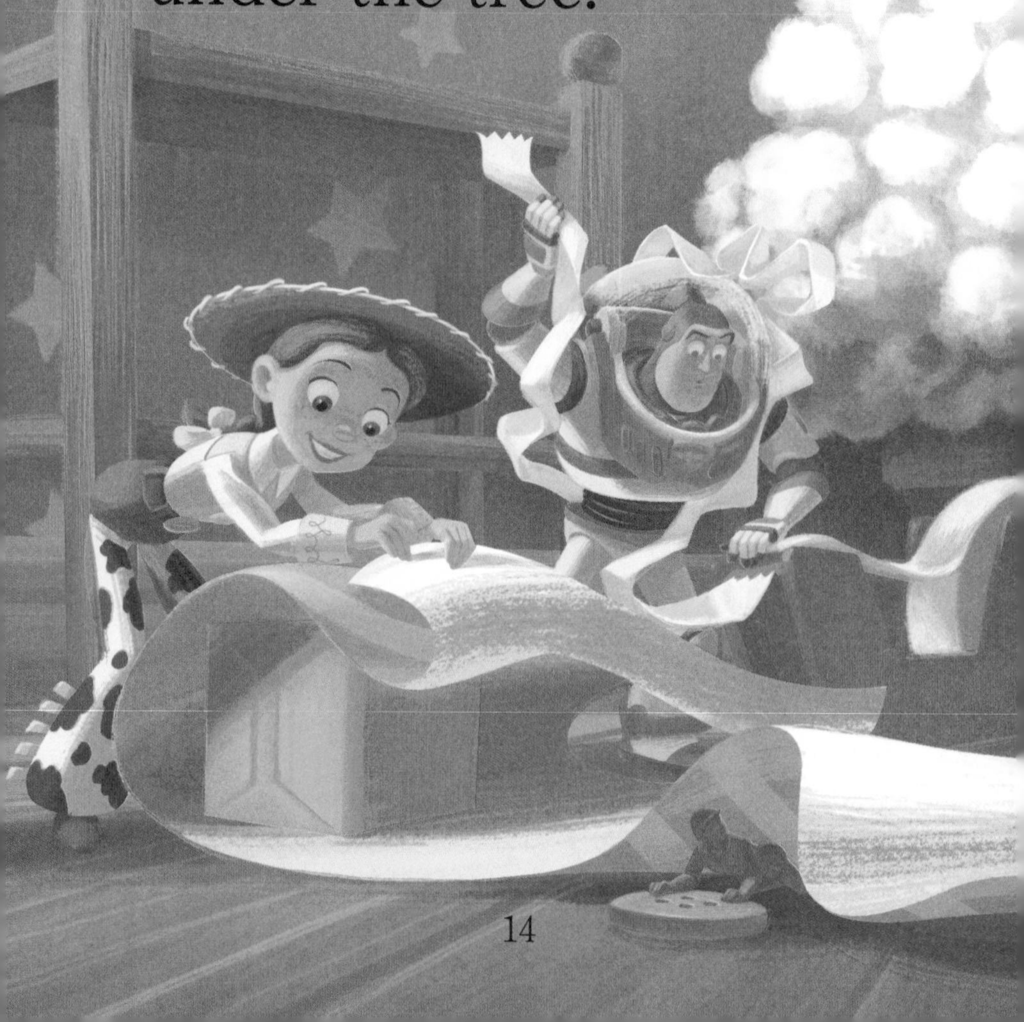

The Green Army Men
and the Aliens
add ribbons and bows.

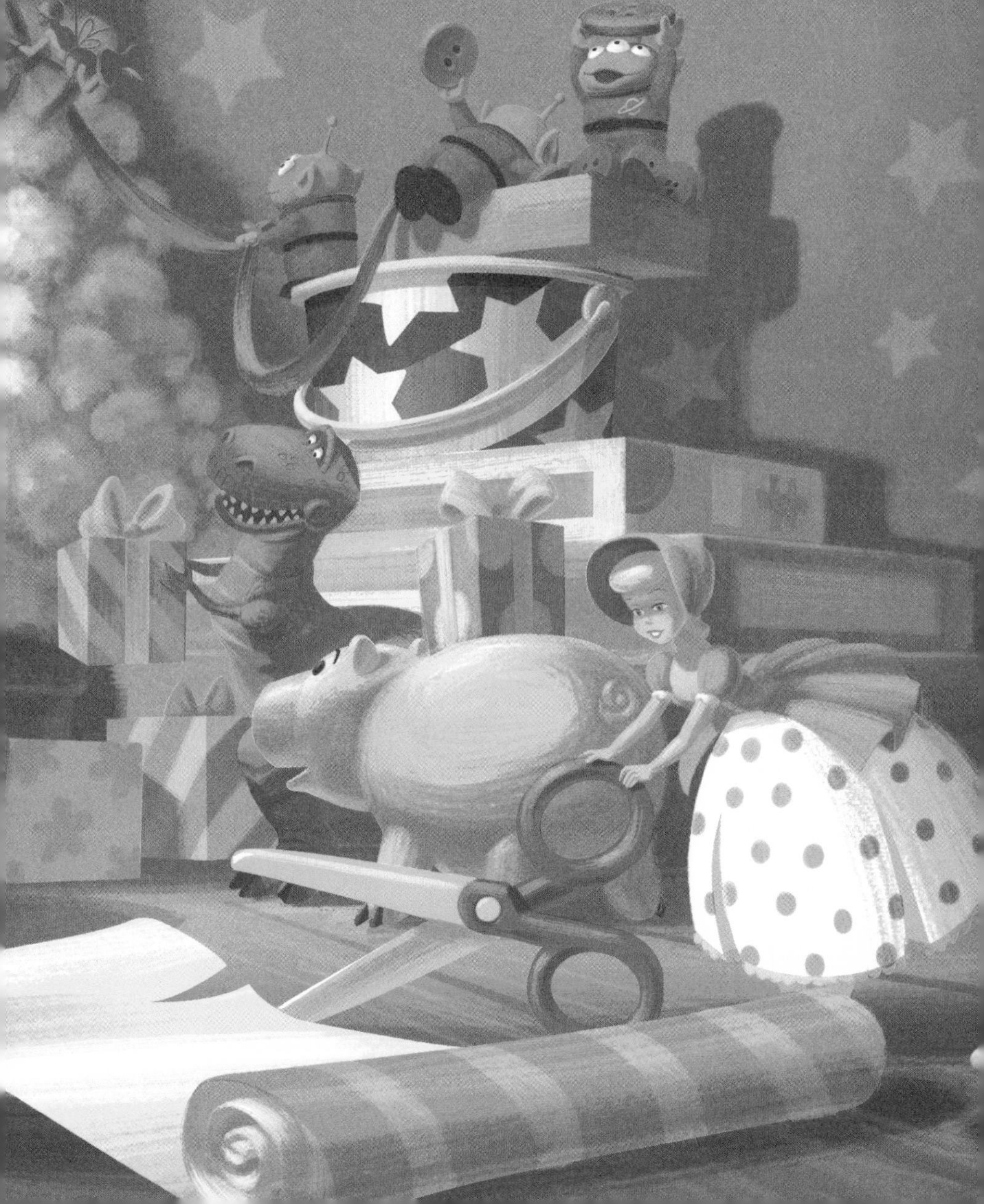

Jessie makes
a Santa hat
for Rex.

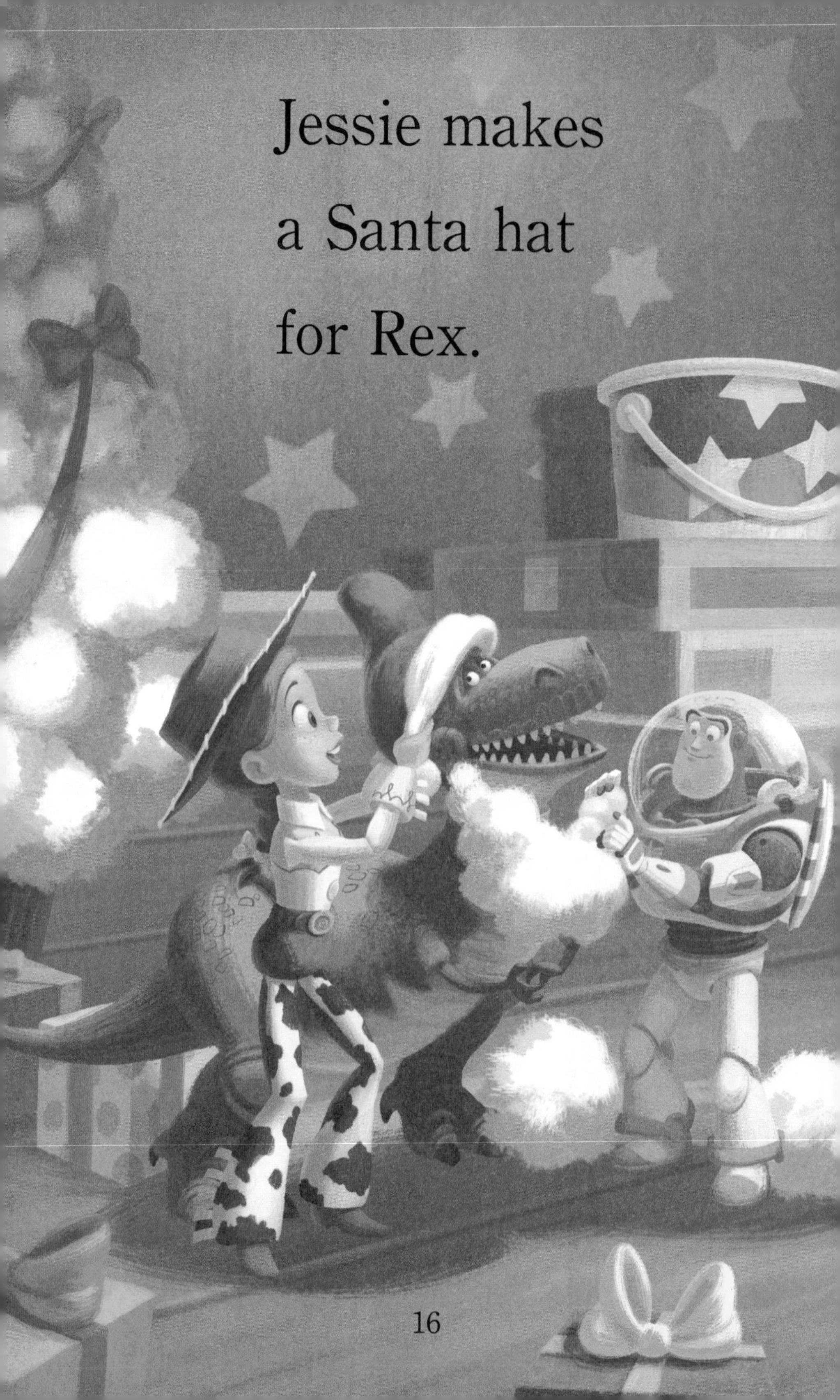

Buzz makes Rex a beard.
The Green Army Men
turn RC into a sled.

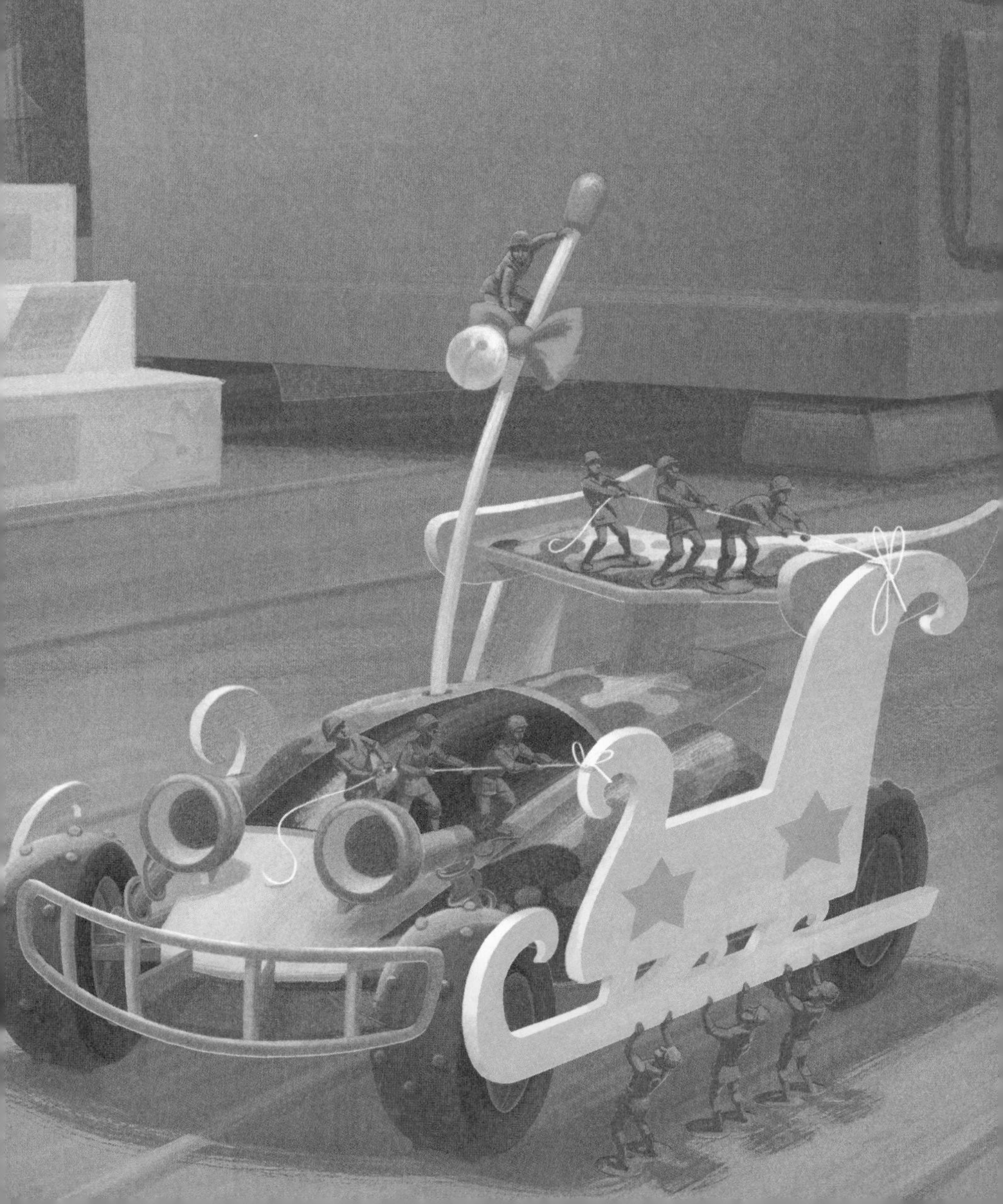

It is Christmas Eve.

Woody still misses Andy.

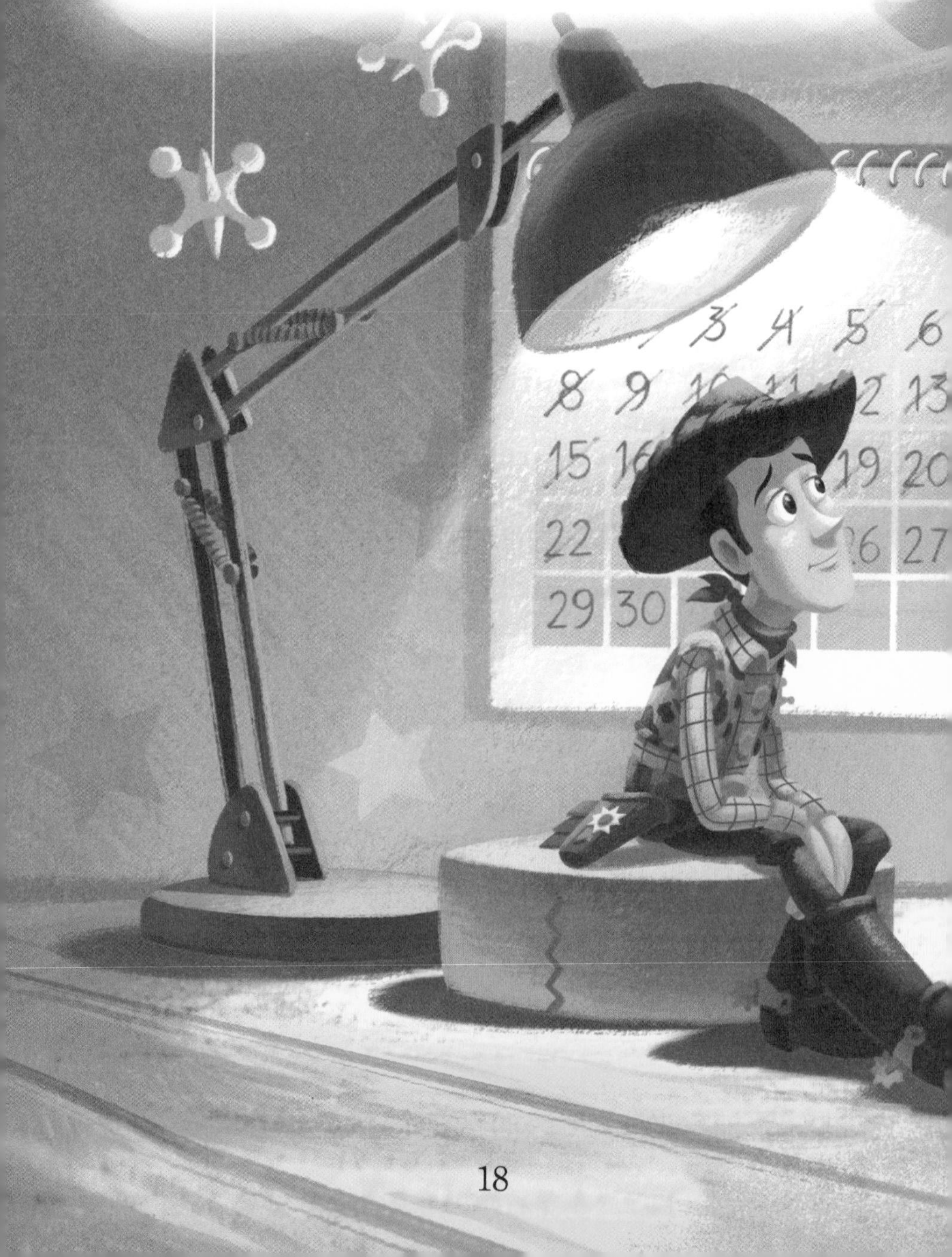

Buzz tells Woody
that his friends have
a Christmas surprise!

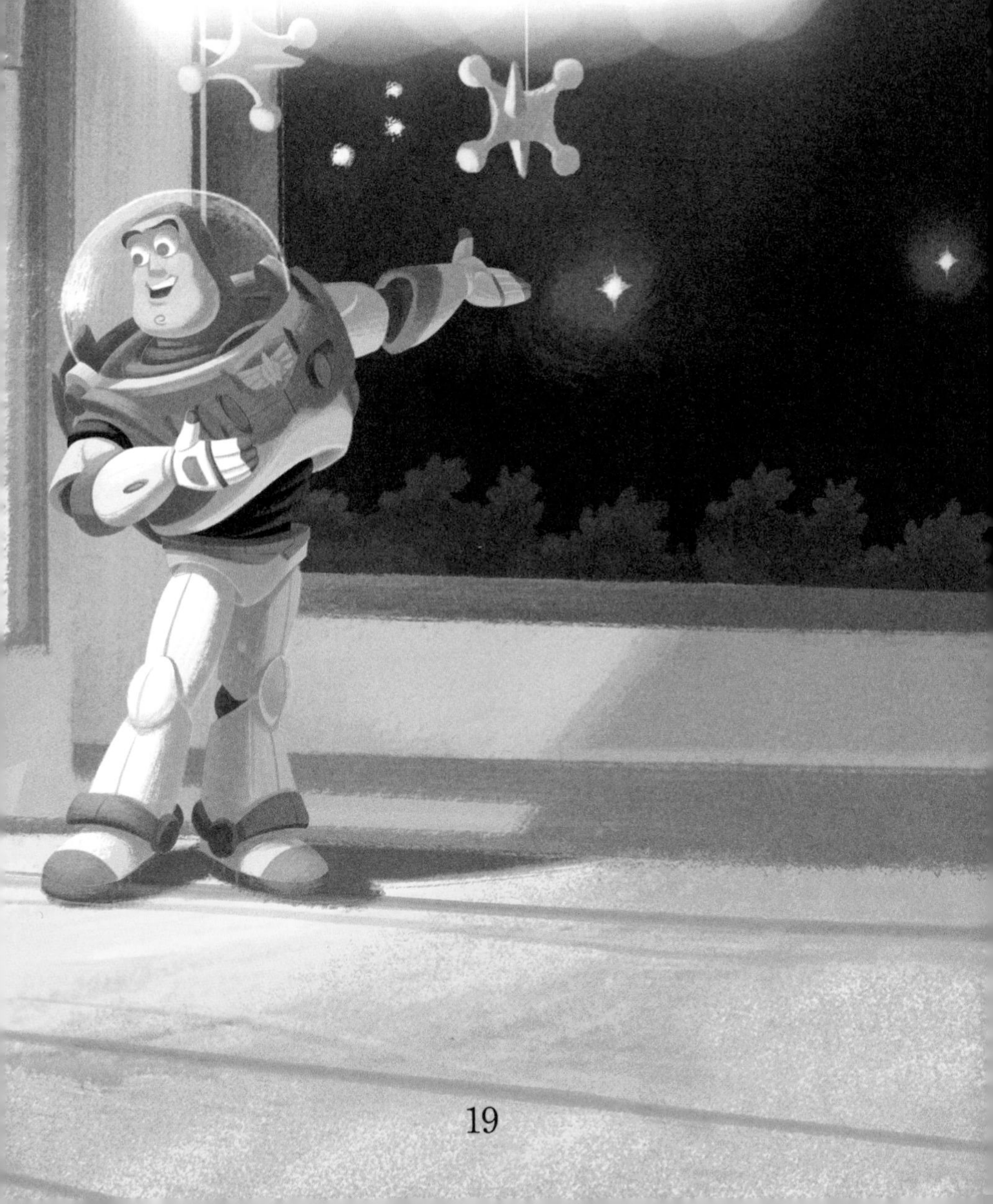

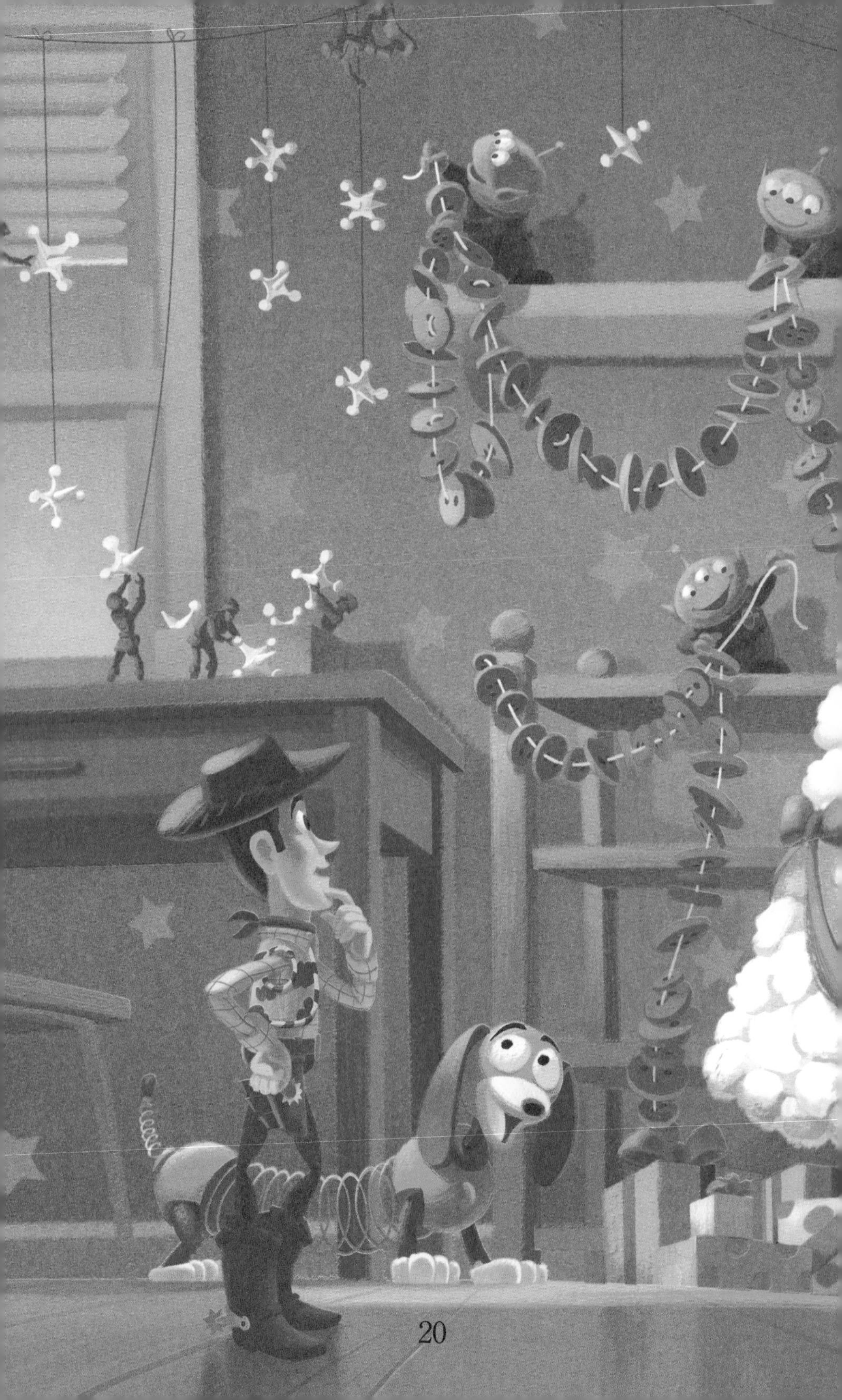

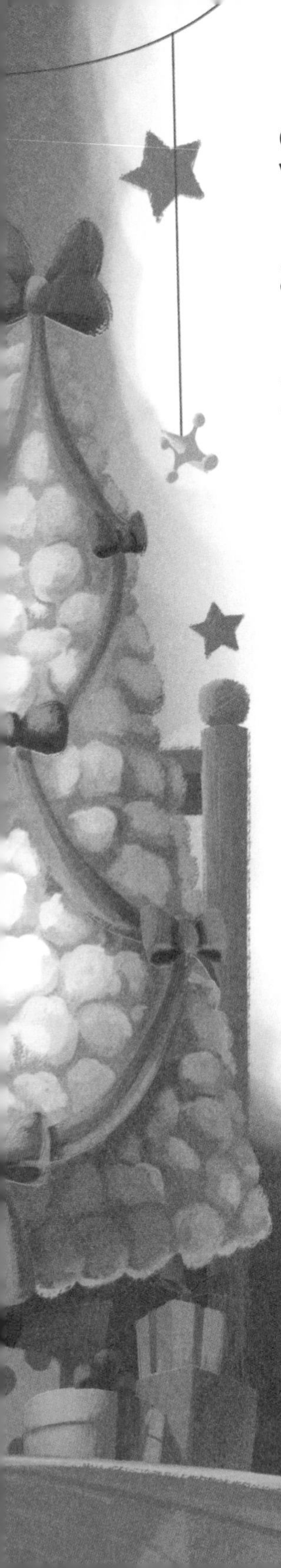

Slinky shows Woody
a Christmas tree
made of cotton balls!
The Aliens
hang buttons.
The Green Army Men
make snowflakes
out of jacks.

Wheezy sings
Christmas carols
to Woody.

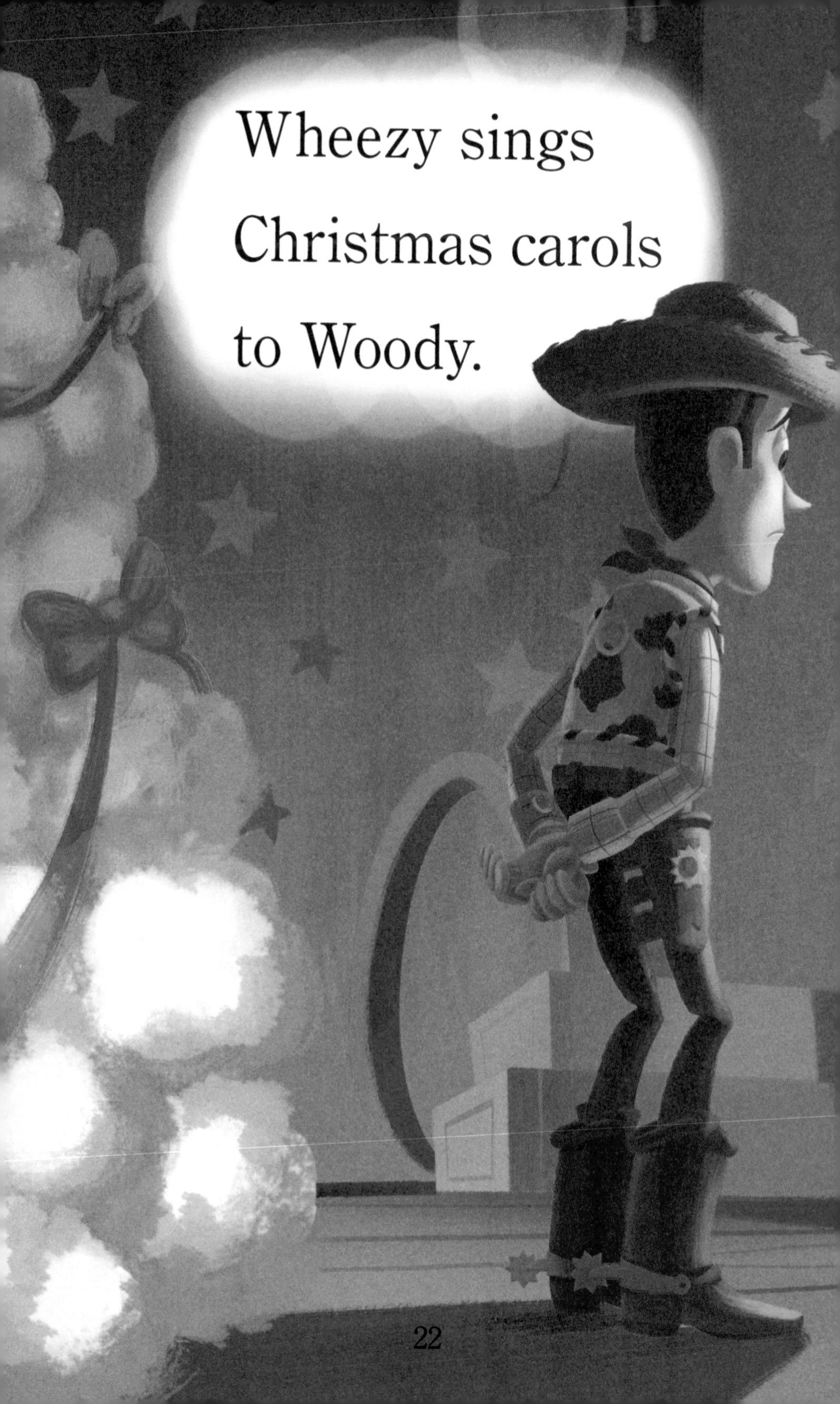

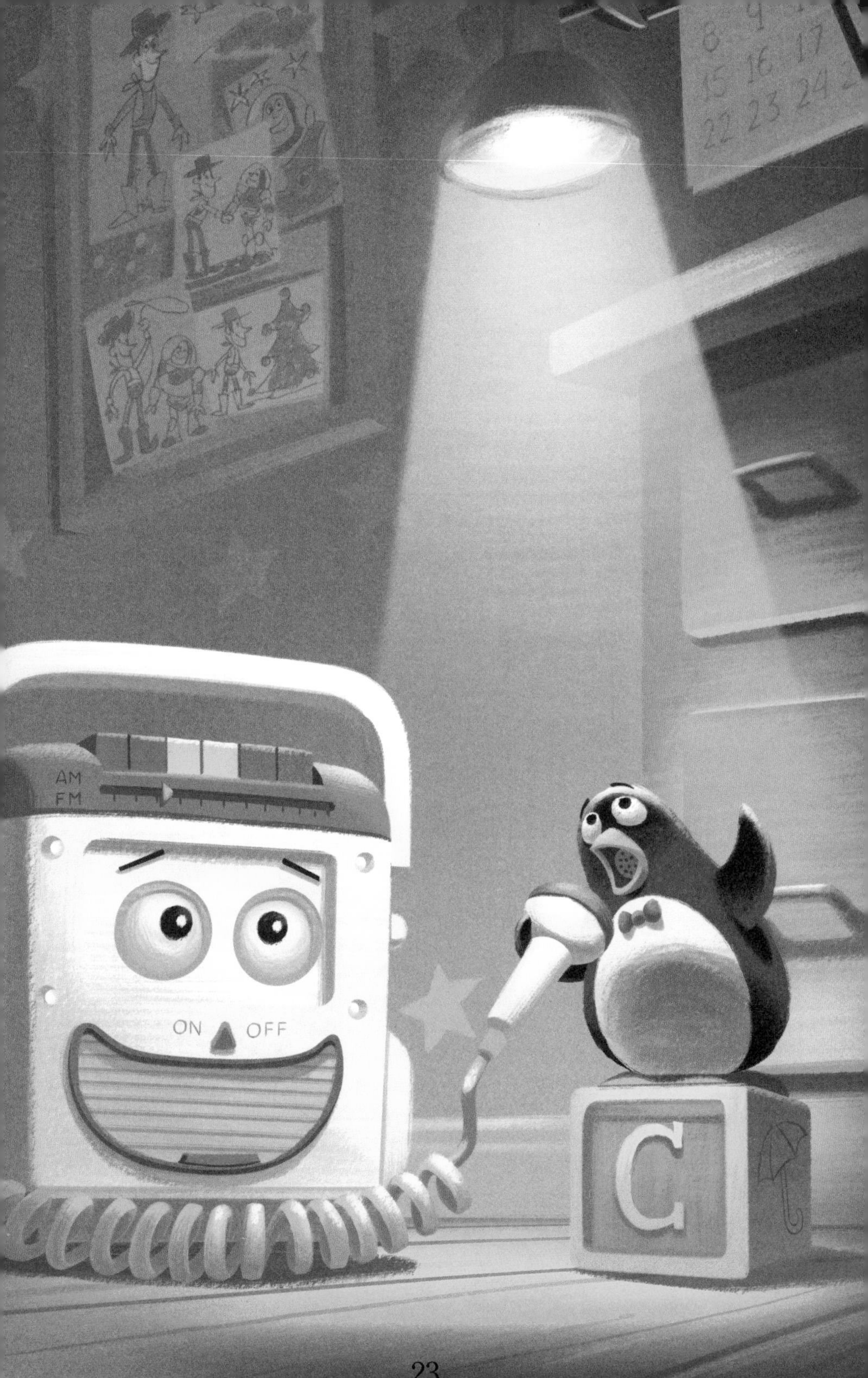
AM
FM
ON
OFF
C

Jessie ties bows.
She hangs them
on the mantel.

Bo Peep reads
a Christmas story
to the toys.

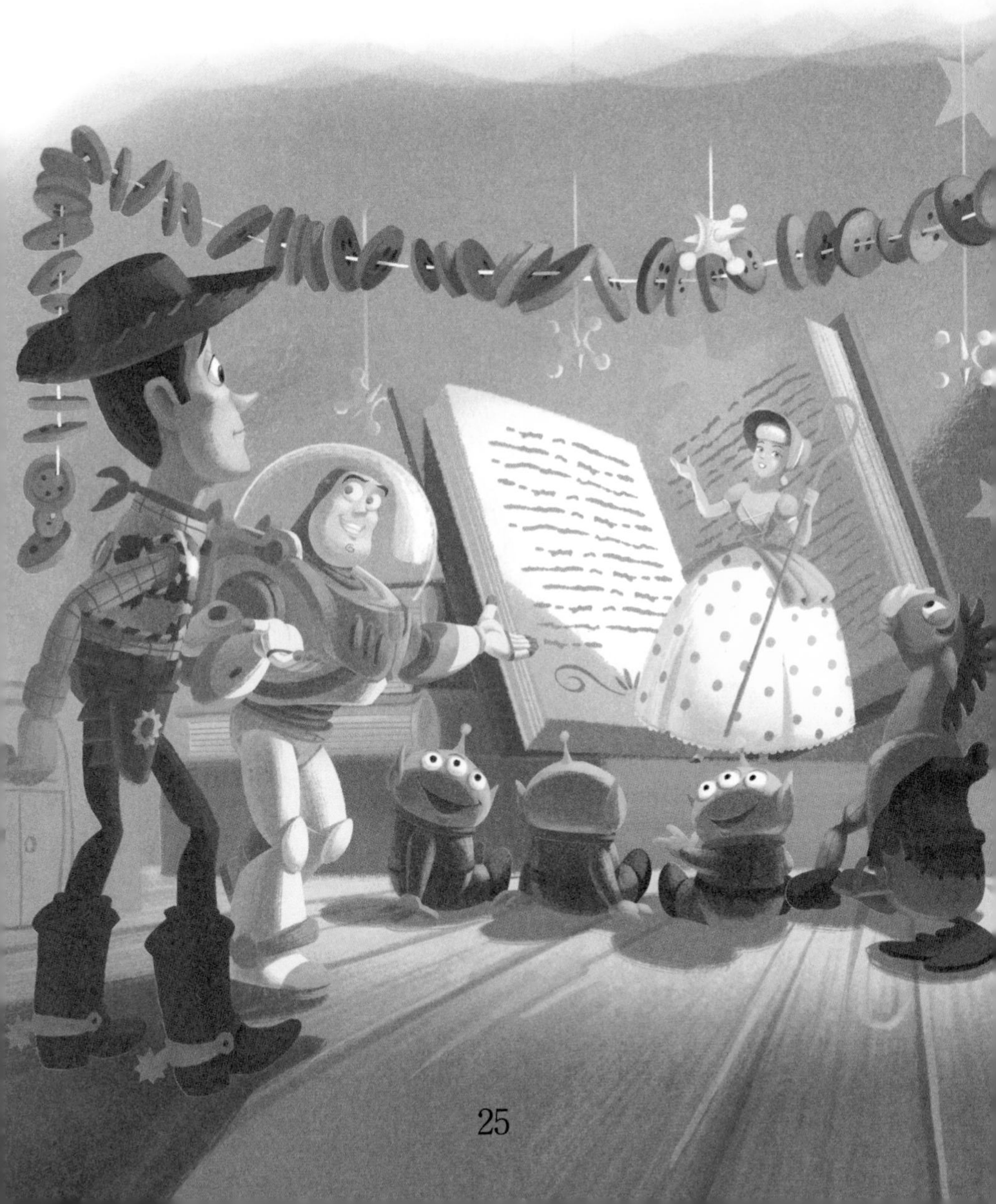

The toys gather
by the Christmas tree.

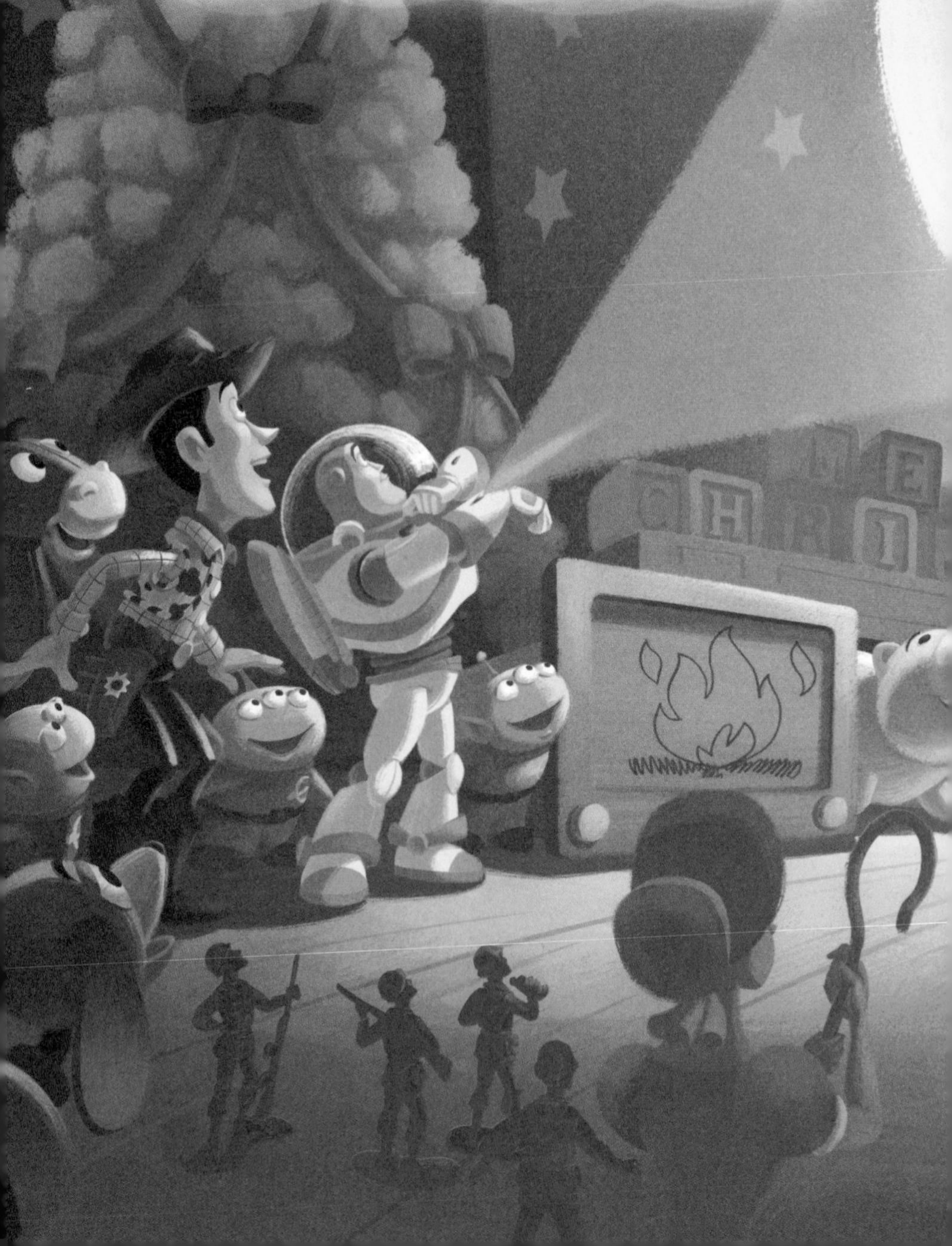

Buzz makes
a light show
with his laser beam!
The toys cheer.
It is Christmas magic!

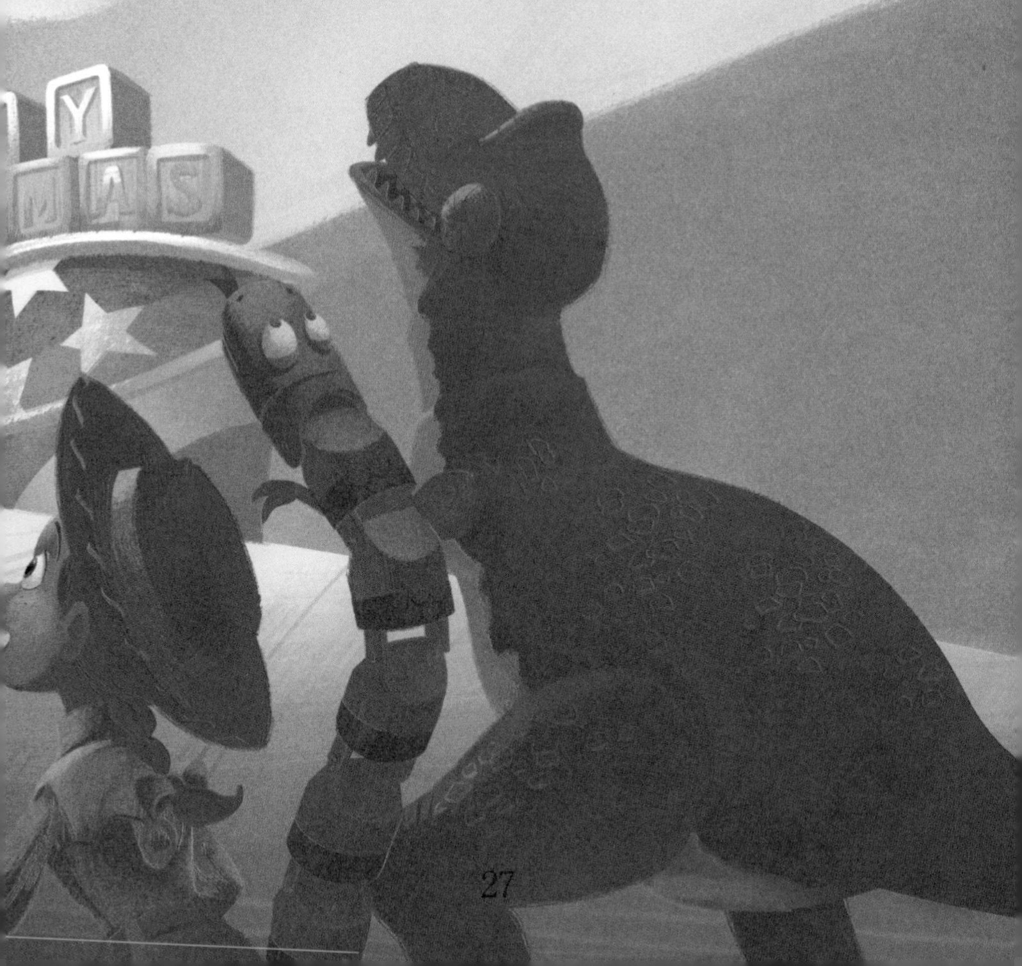

Rex and RC are ready to give out the presents!

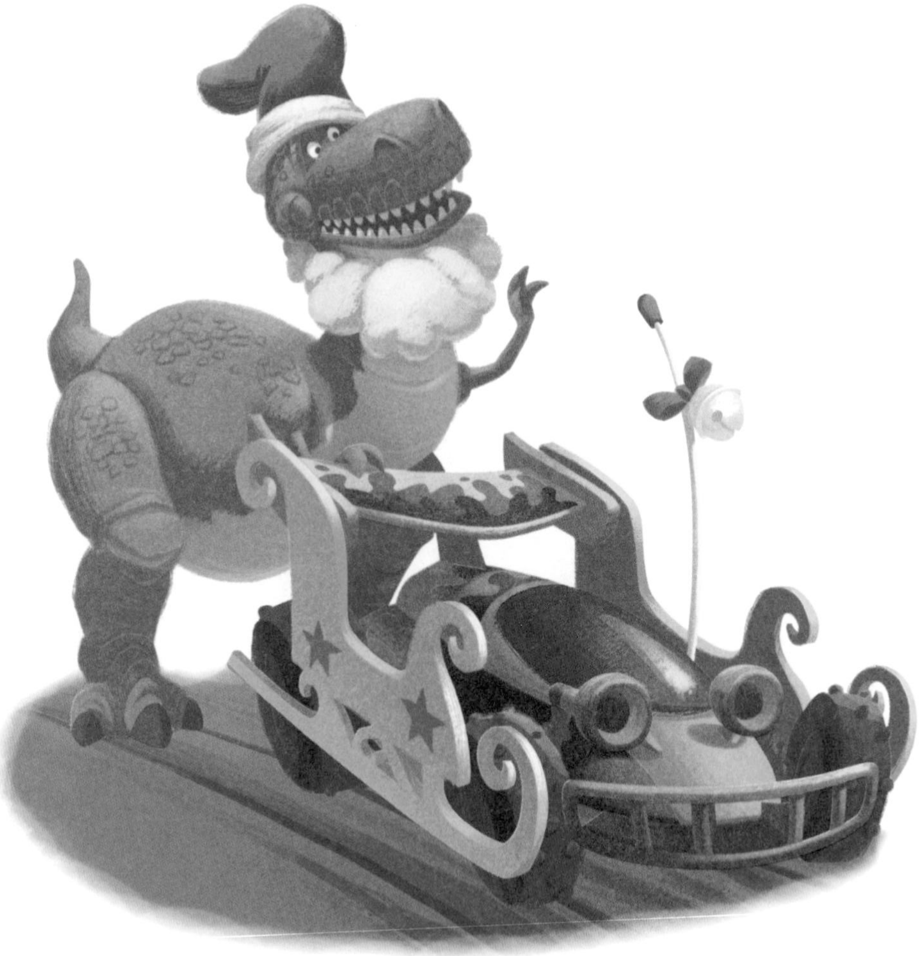

Jessie gives Hamm
a shiny quarter.
Hamm gives Jessie
a doll's dress.
Bo Peep gives Woody
a Christmas kiss.

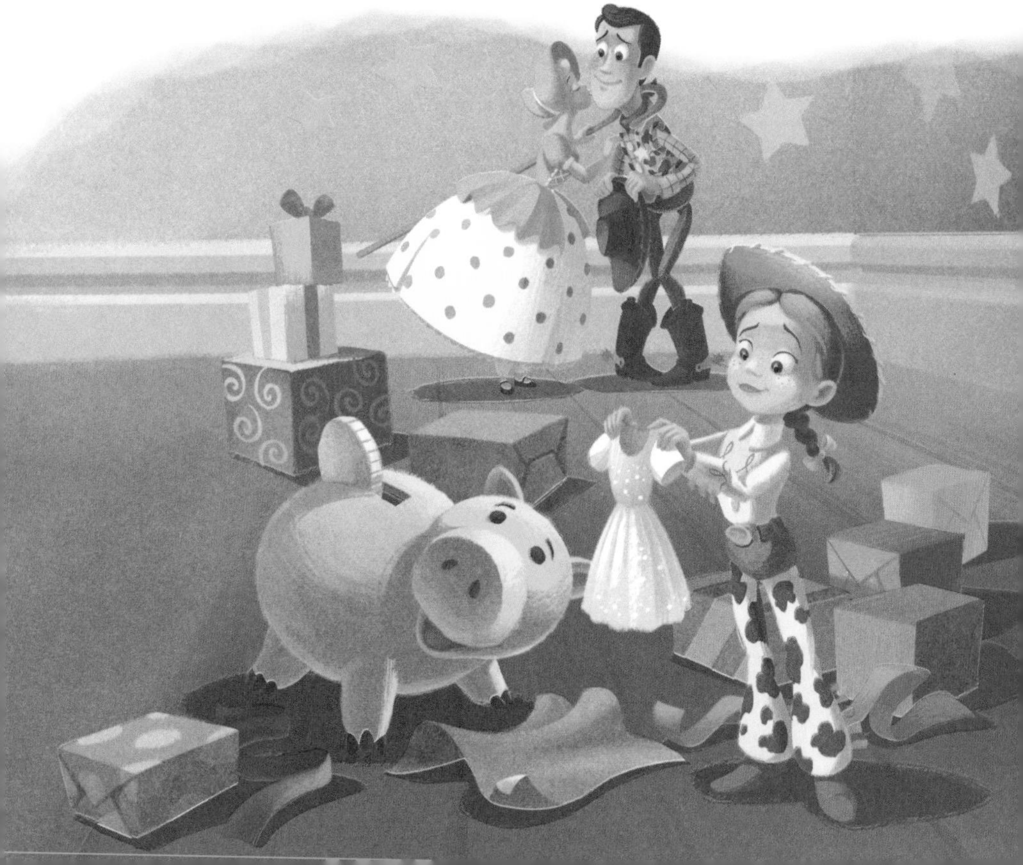

The toys gather

around the tree.

They sing carols.

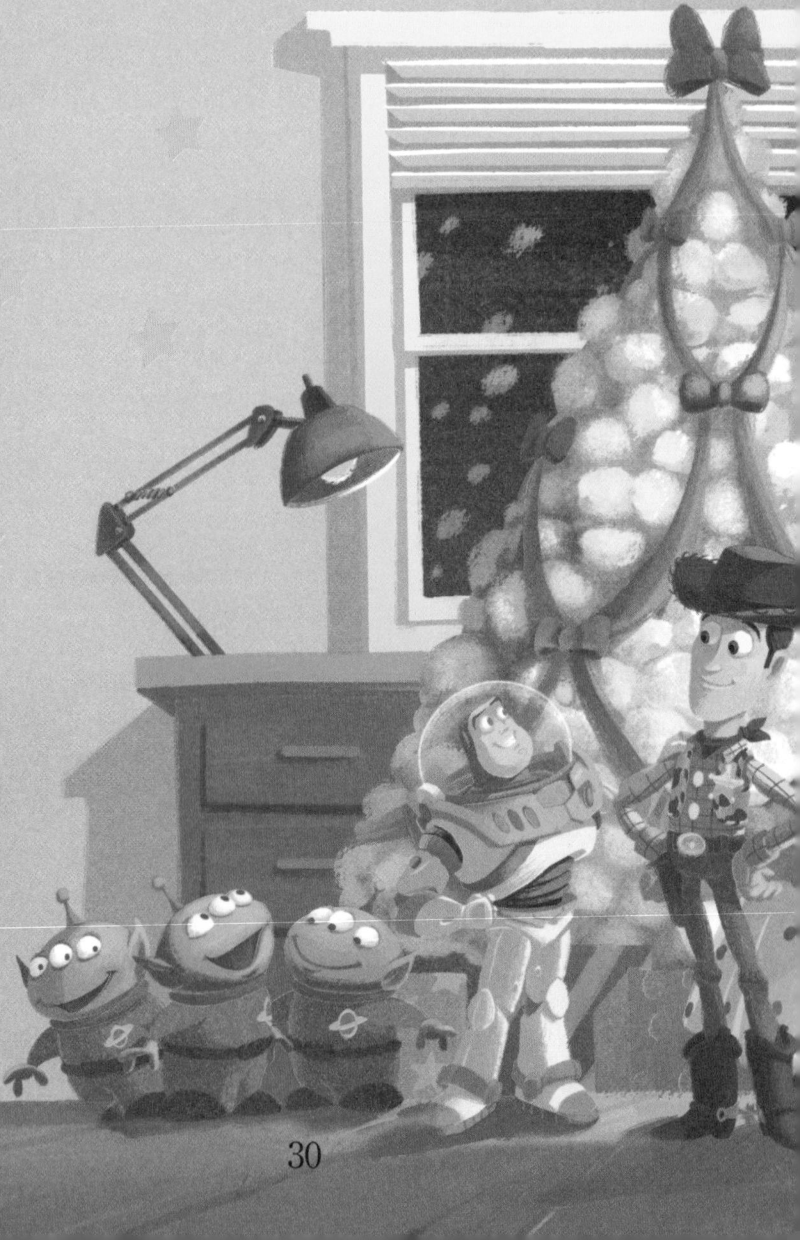

Woody is happy
to spend Christmas
with his friends.
He wishes them all
a merry Christmas.

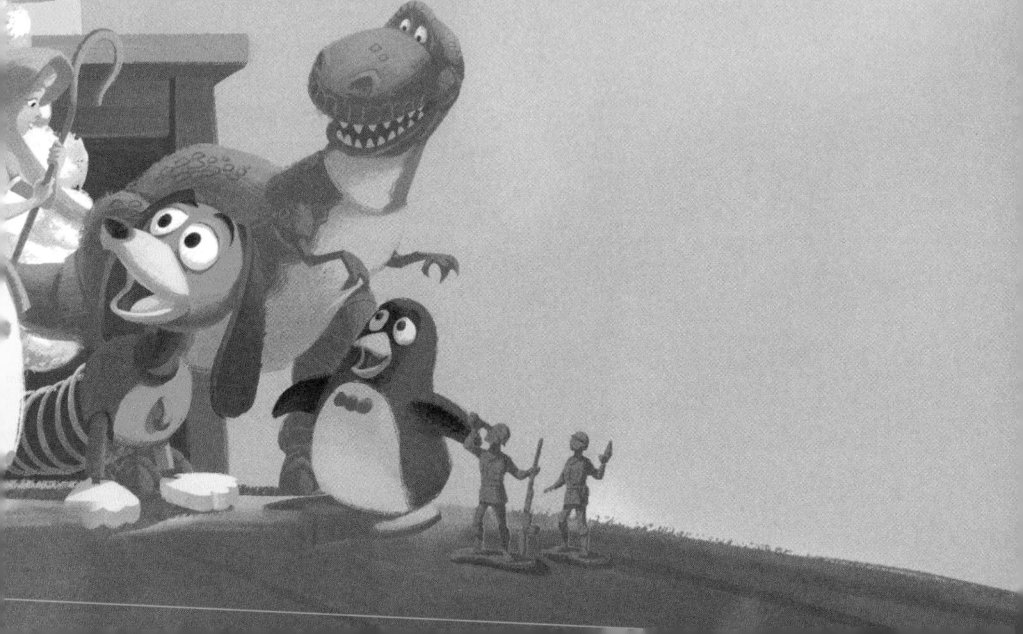

The toys look
out the window.
Snow!
It is good to be
with friends
on Christmas!

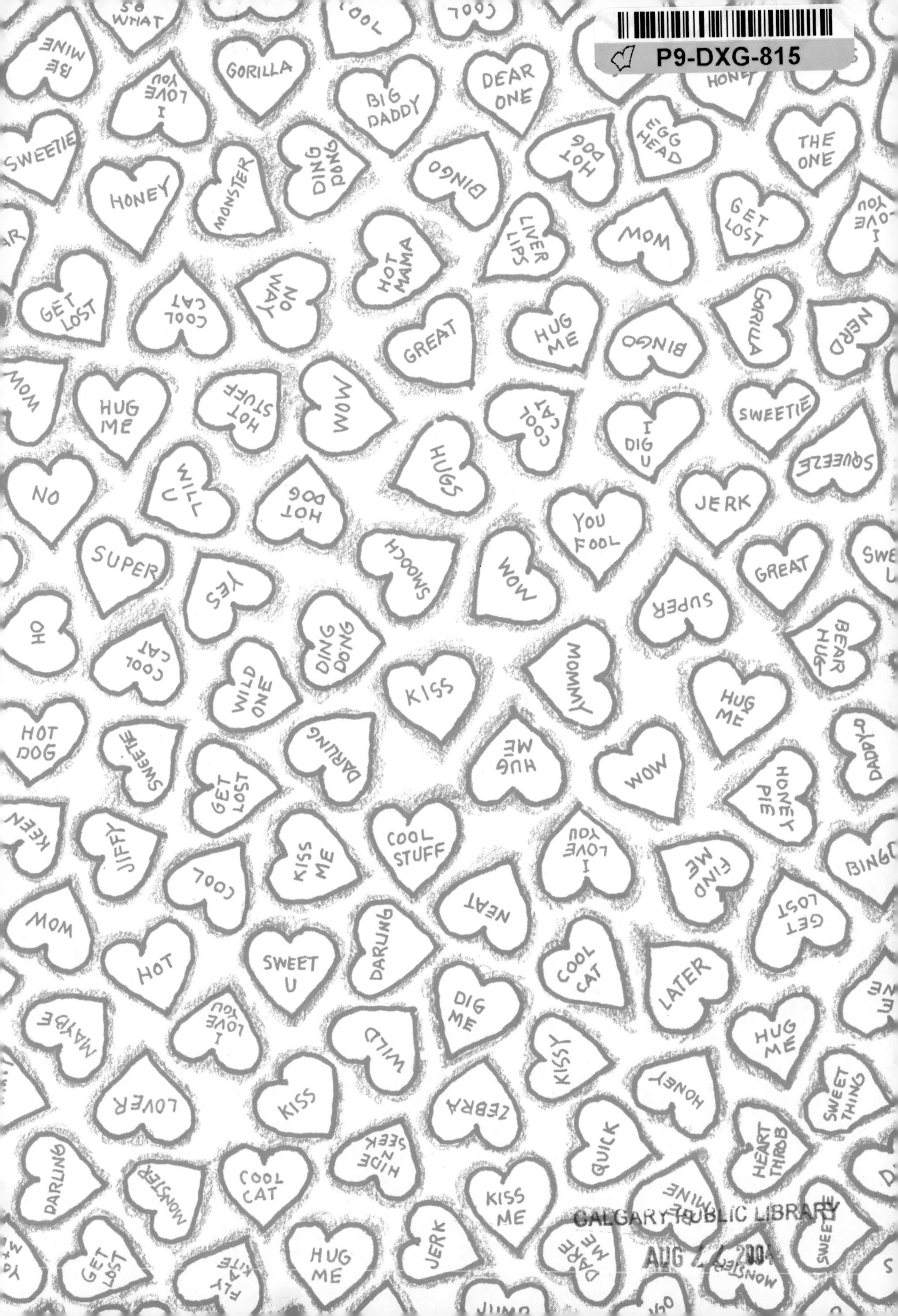
SO WHAT
COOL
COOL
BE MINE
GORILLA
I LOVE YOU
DEAR ONE
BIG DADDY
HONEY
SWEETIE
EGG HEAD
HOT DOG
THE ONE
DING DONG
BINGO
HONEY
MONSTER
LIVER LIPS
MOM
GET LOST
I LOVE YOU
HOT MAMA
GET LOST
COOL CAT
NO WAY
GREAT
HUG ME
BINGO
GORILLA
NERD
WOW
HUG ME
HOT STUFF
WOW
COOL CAT
I DIG U
SWEETIE
SQUEEZE
HUGS
NO
WILL U
HOT DOG
JERK
YOU FOOL
SUPER
YES
SMOOCH
WOW
GREAT
SUPER
OH
COOL CAT
DING DONG
WILD ONE
MOMMY
BEAR HUG
KISS
HUG ME
HOT DOG
SWEETIE
DARLING
HUG ME
WOW
DADDY-O
GET LOST
HONEY PIE
KEEN
JIFFY
KISS ME
COOL STUFF
I LOVE YOU
FIND ME
COOL
NEAT
GET LOST
MOM
DARLING
HOT
SWEET U
COOL CAT
LATER
MAYBE
I LOVE YOU
DIG ME
WILD
KISSY
HUG ME
LOVER
KISS
ZEBRA
HONEY
SWEET THING
QUICK
HEART THROB
DARLING
HIDE N SEEK
MONSTER
COOL CAT
KISS ME
BE MINE
GET LOST
JERK
HUG ME
DARE ME
FLY KITE

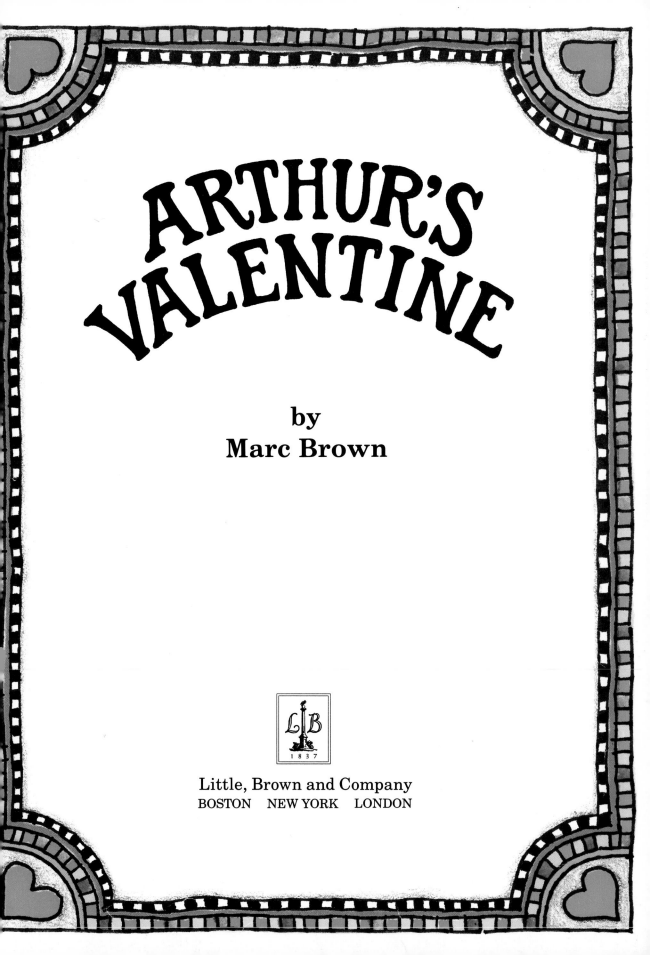

ARTHUR'S VALENTINE

by
Marc Brown

Little, Brown and Company
BOSTON   NEW YORK   LONDON

For Melanie, Lyn,
and Felice—
all of whom
I regard with
wonder and delight

Republished in 1987

Library of Congress Cataloging-in-Publication Data
Brown, Marc Tolon.
  Arthur's valentine.

Arthur® is a registered trademark of Marc Brown.

  Summary: Arthur's wrong guess about the identity of the secret
admirer sending him valentine messages leads to teasing by the other
children, but clues in additional messages allow him to get his due.
  [1. St. Valentine's Day—Fiction. 2. Animals—Fiction] I. Title.
PZ7.B81618As   [E]   80-14001
ISBN 0-316-11062-0 (hc)
ISBN 0-316-11187-2 (pbk)

HC: 20 19 18 17
PB: 25 24 23 22

WOR

Printed in the United States of America

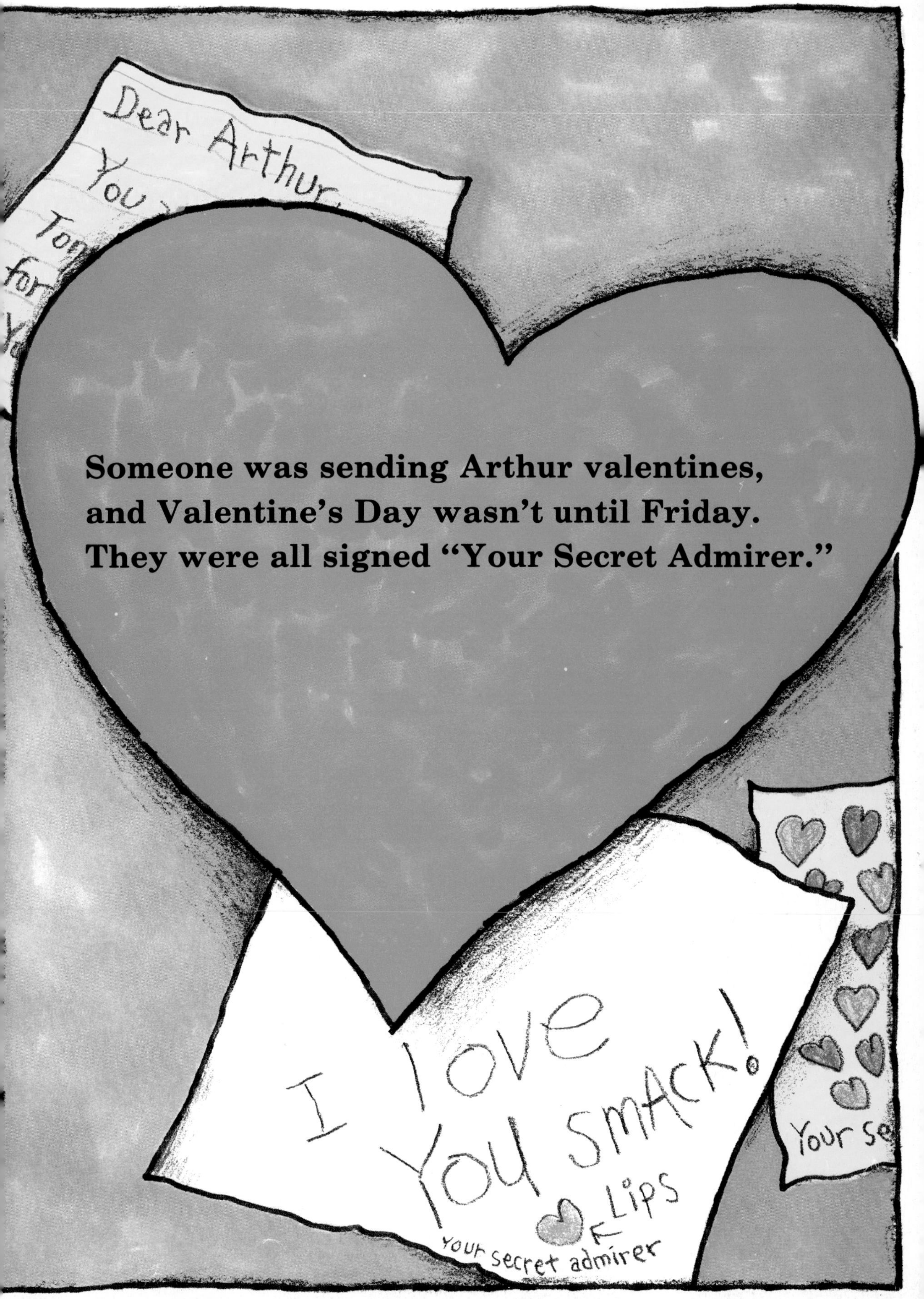
Dear Arthur,
You
I love You SMACK!
Lips
your secret admirer

Someone was sending Arthur valentines, and Valentine's Day wasn't until Friday. They were all signed "Your Secret Admirer."

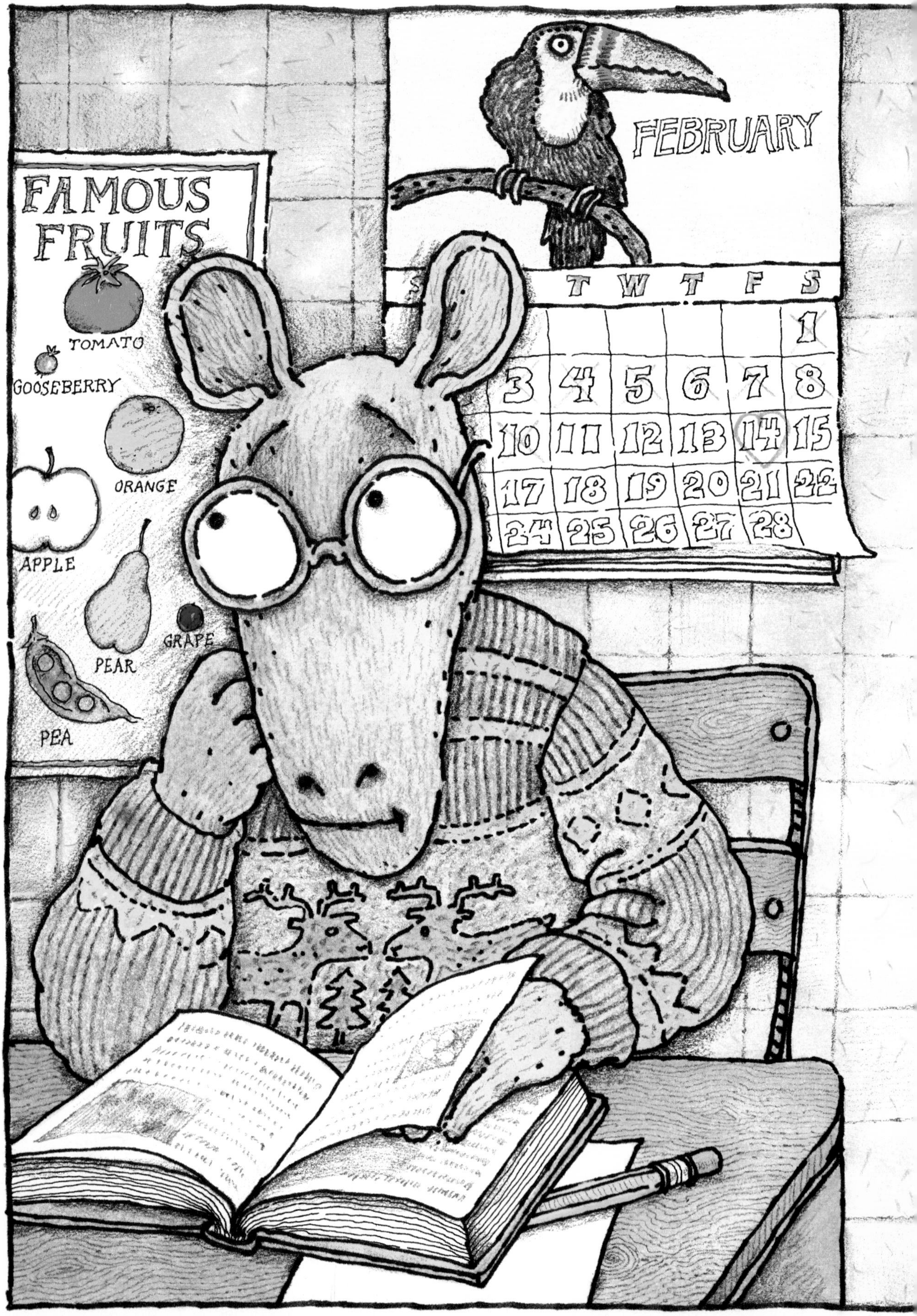
FAMOUS FRUITS
TOMATO
GOOSEBERRY
ORANGE
APPLE
PEAR
GRAPE
PEA
FEBRUARY
T W T F S
1
3 4 5 6 7 8
10 11 12 13 14 15
17 18 19 20 21 22
24 25 26 27 28

It was a real mystery.
Who was Arthur's secret admirer?
It might be Fern.

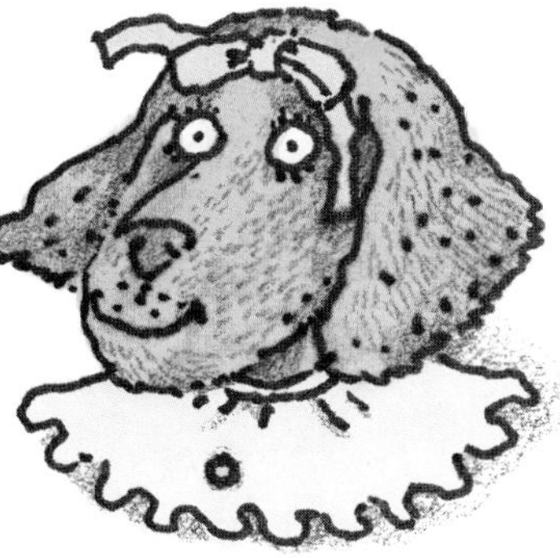

It could be Buster playing a joke.

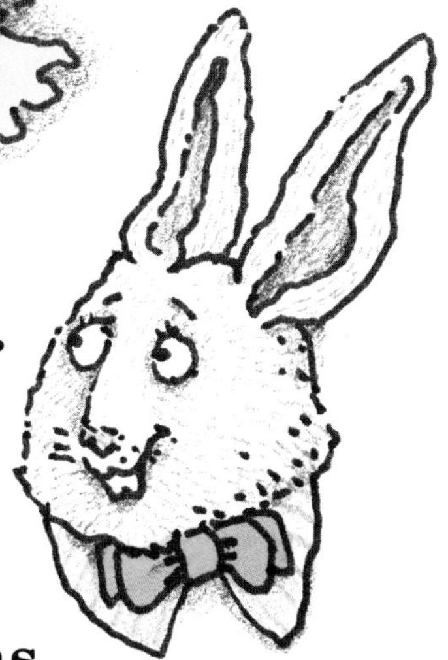

Or maybe even Francine. She was always teasing Arthur.

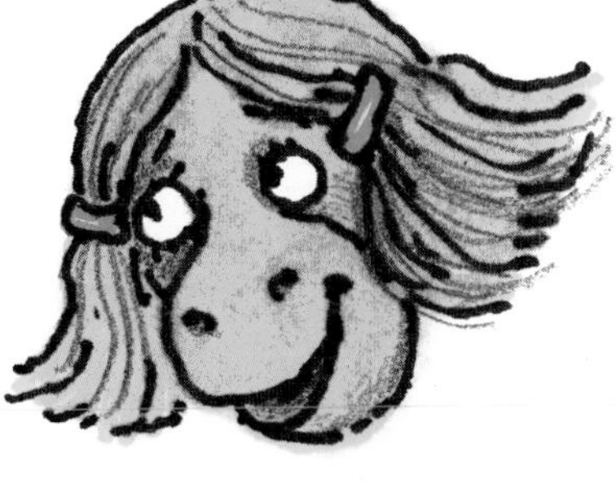

Arthur hoped it was the new girl, Sue Ellen.

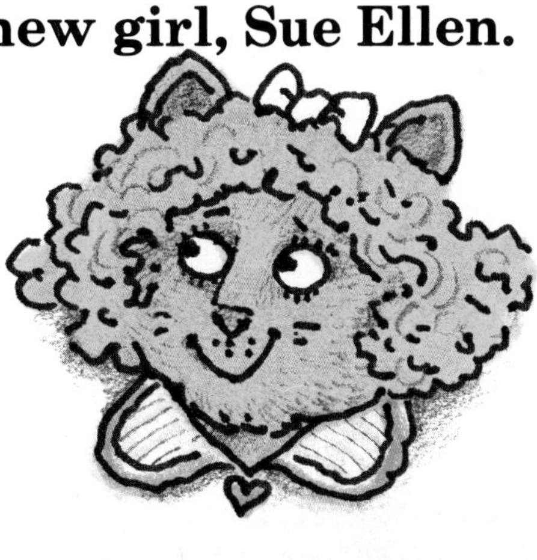

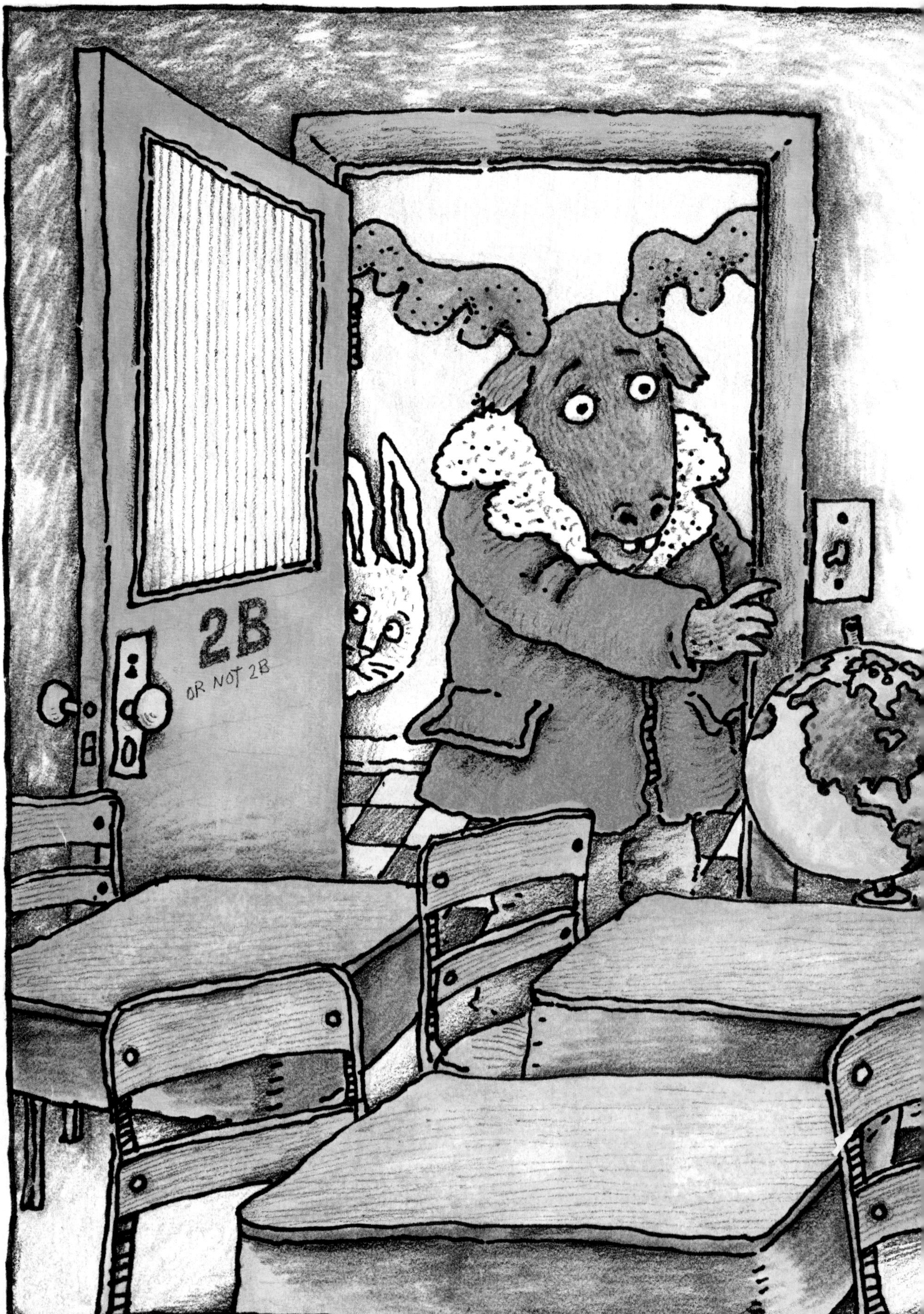
2B
OR NOT 2B

On Wednesday, Arthur found a new valentine.

Apples, Bananas, Peaches, a Pear,
With a face like yours,
You're lucky I care.
Your Secret Admirer
P.S. In your lunch box you'll find a treat.
It's just for you and it's extra sweet.

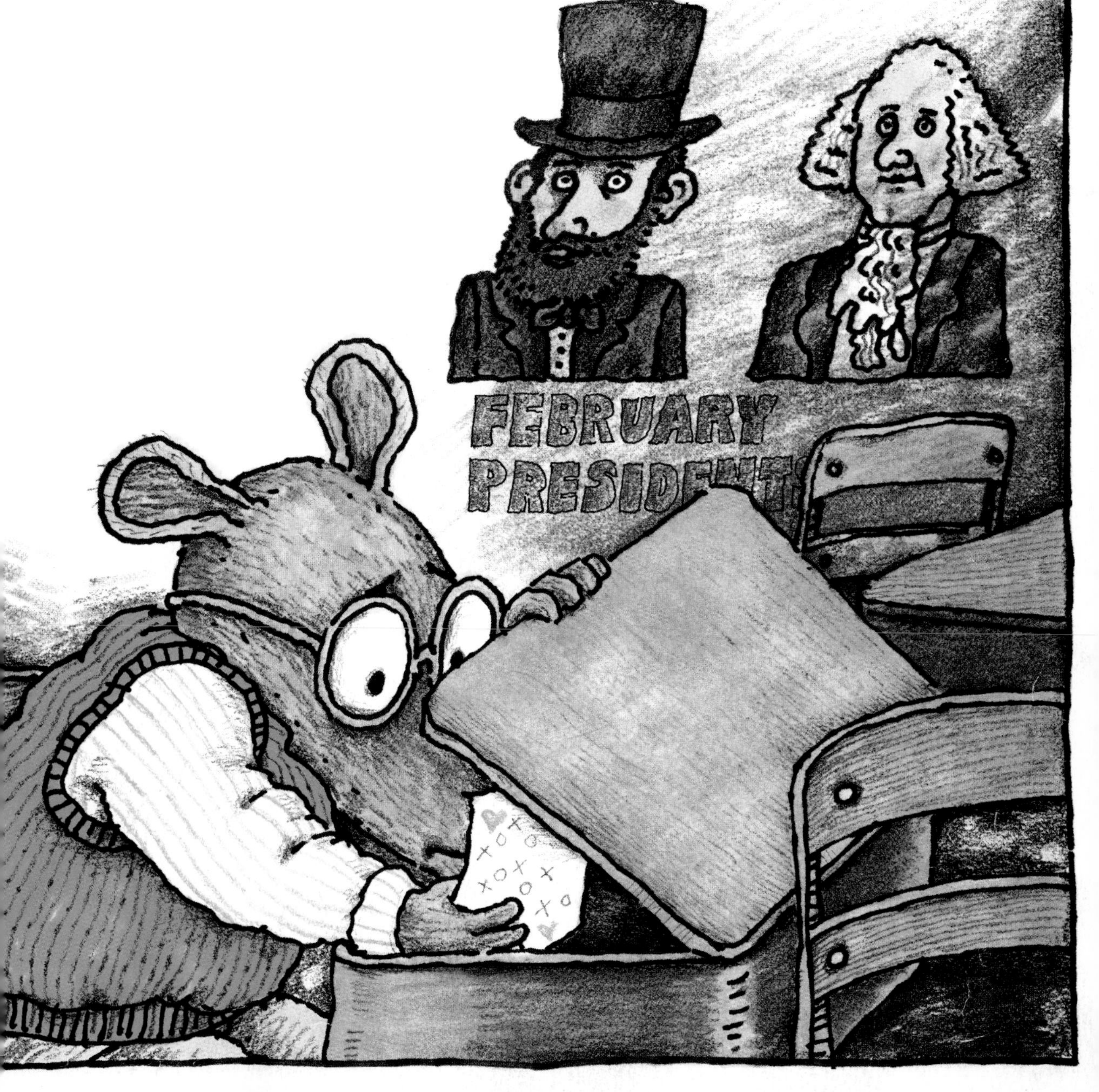
FEBRUARY
PRESIDE

Arthur hoped it might be chocolate, but at lunch he found this note:

Candy is sweet,
Lemons are sour.
I'll be watching you
The whole lunch hour.

Arthur looked at Sue Ellen. She smiled.

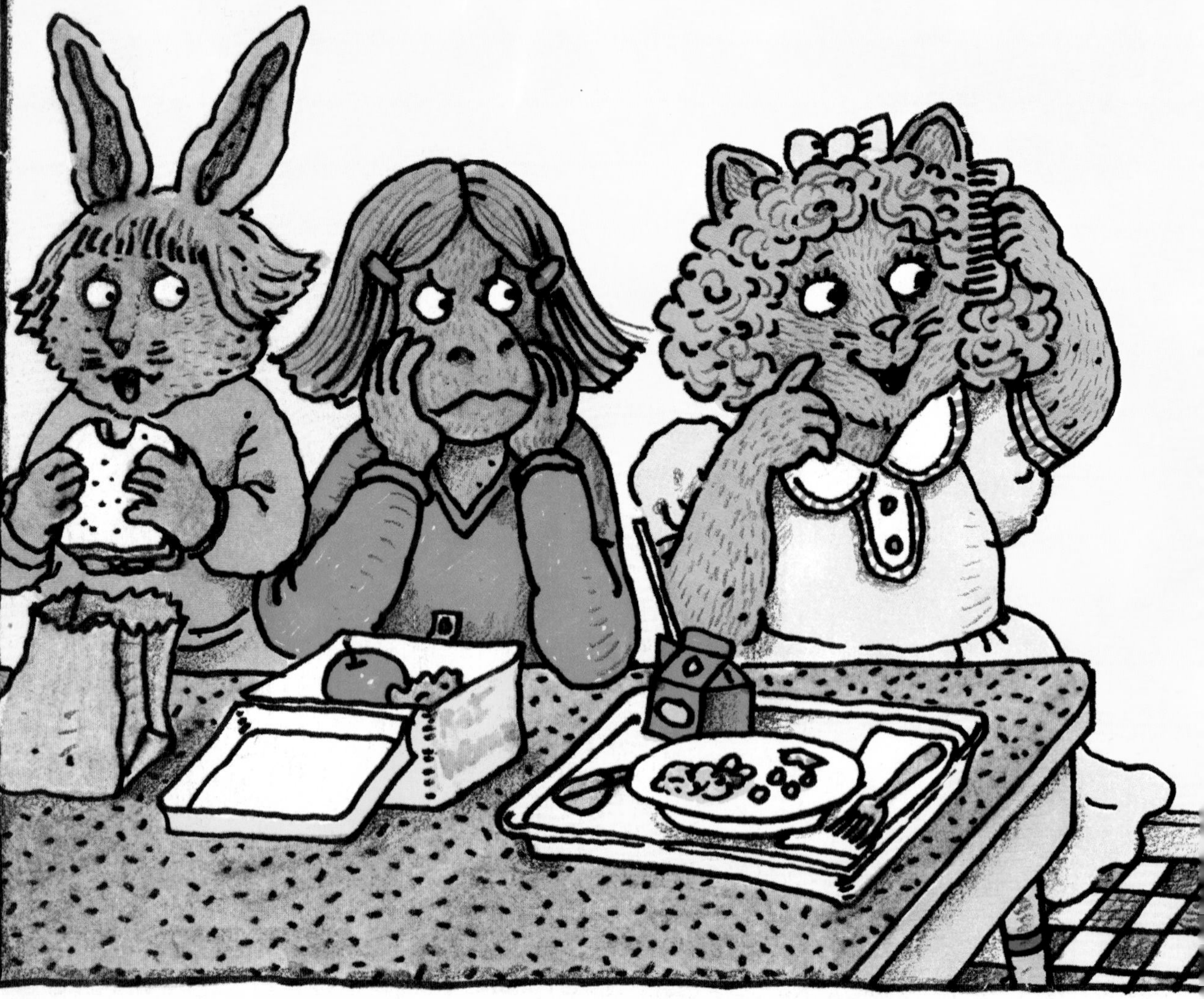

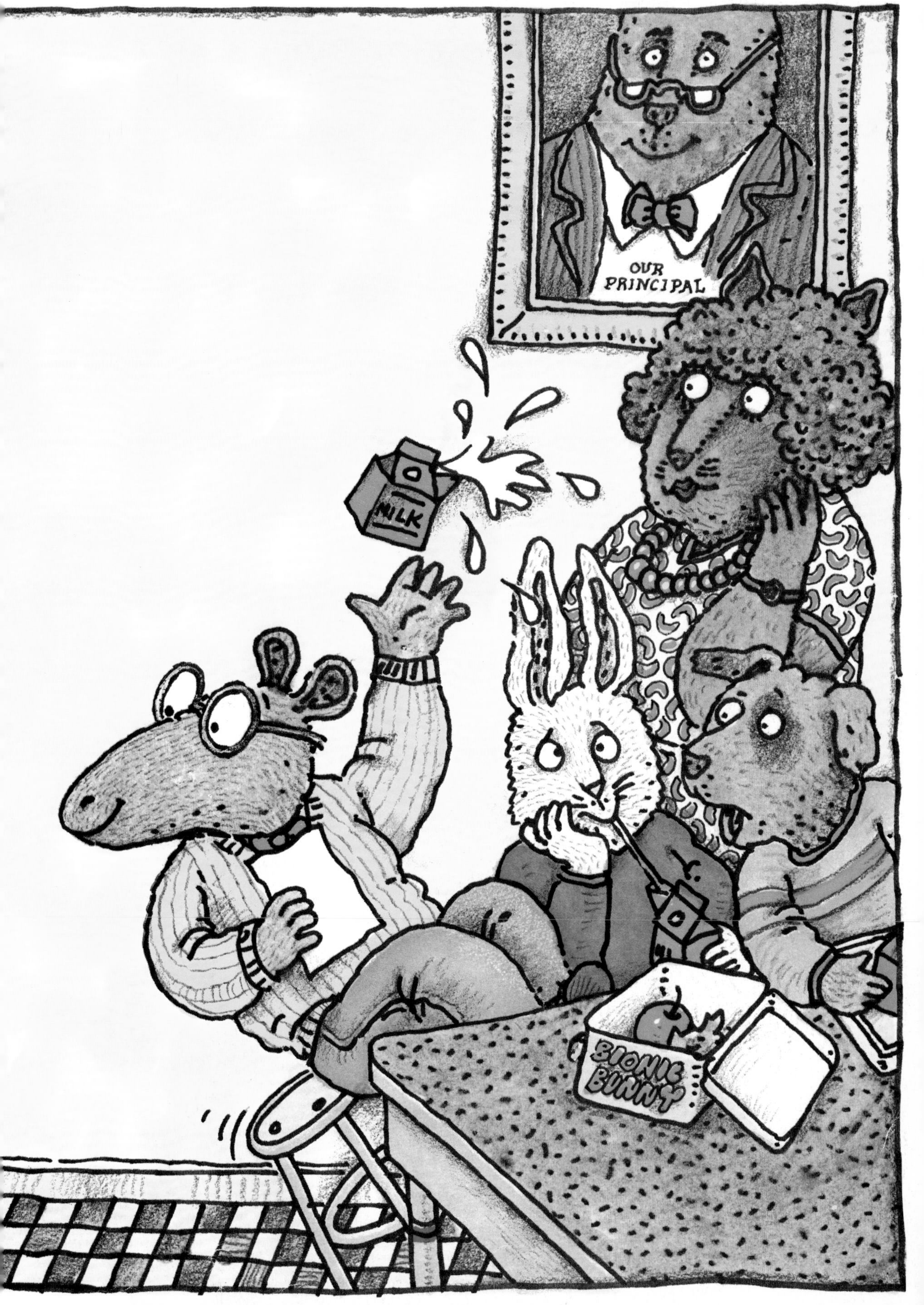
OUR PRINCIPAL
MILK
BIONIC BUNNY

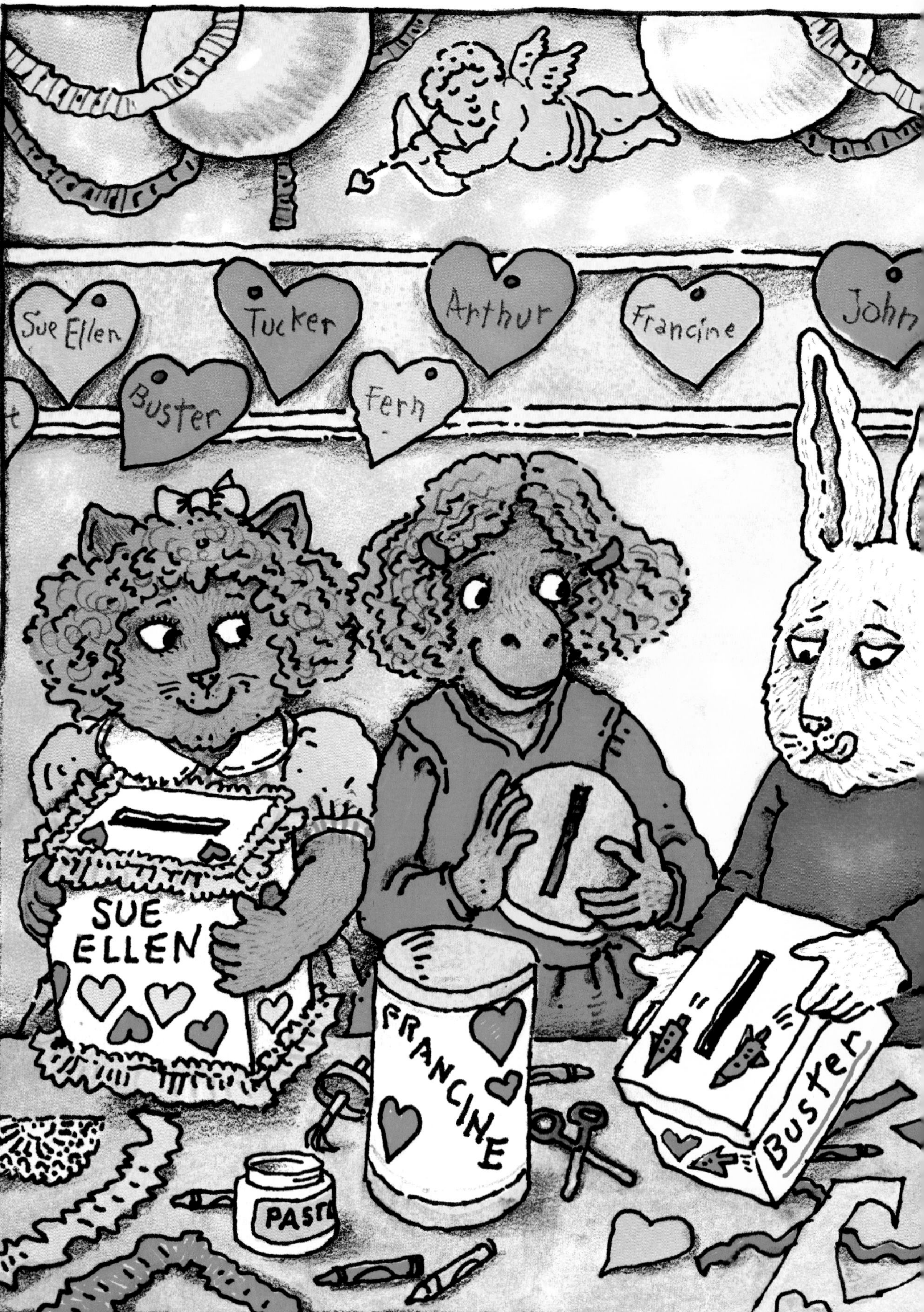
Sue Ellen
Tucker
Arthur
Francine
Buster
Fern
SUE ELLEN
FRANCINE
Buster

Thursday, everyone made valentine boxes. Arthur decided to make a special card instead.

When everyone mailed their valentines, Arthur put his card in Sue Ellen's box.

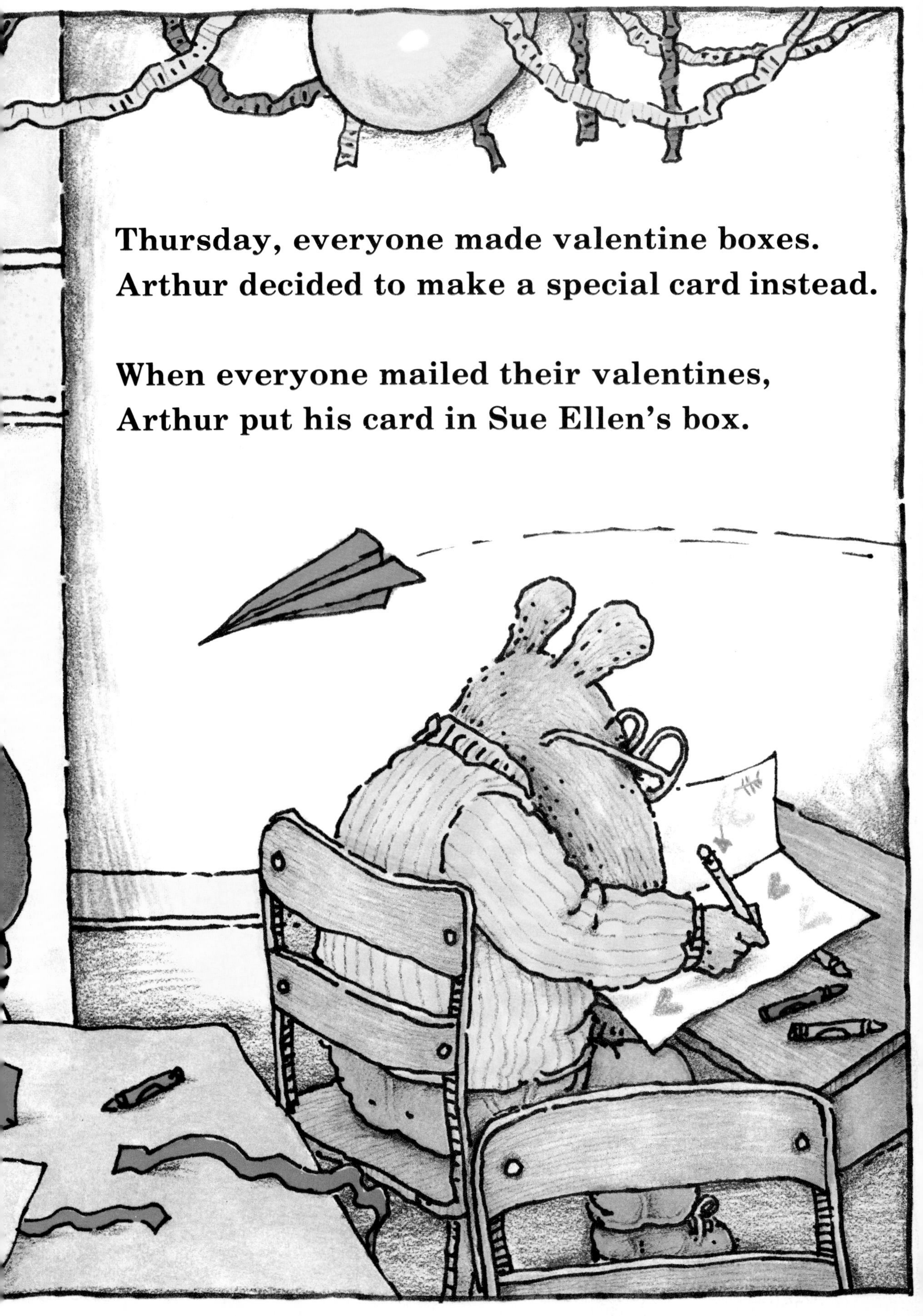

Then, when nobody was looking,
Arthur hid the valentines
from the secret admirer
in his coat pocket.

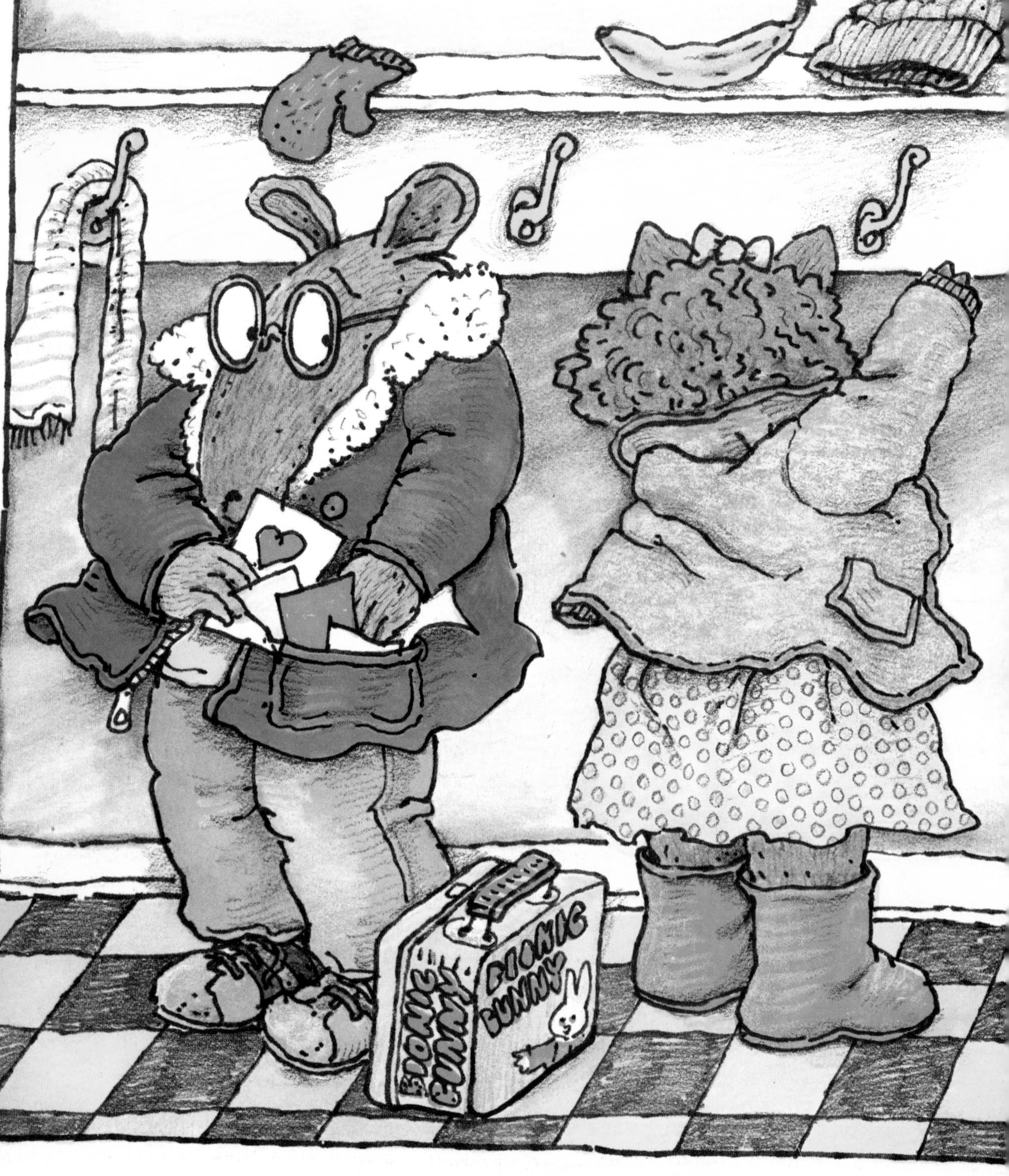
BIONIC BUNNY
BIONIC BUNNY

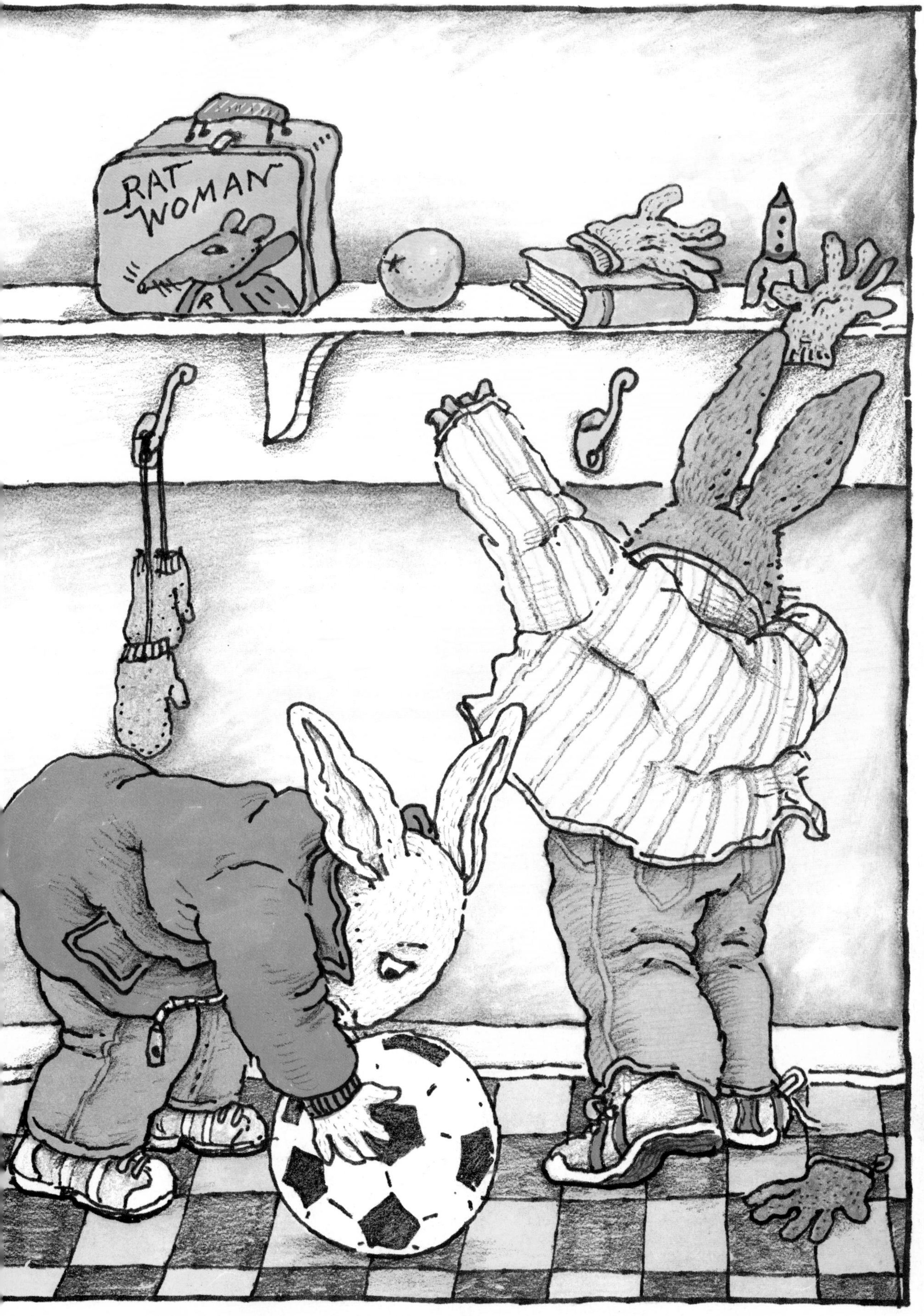
RAT WOMAN
R

After school, Arthur took off his coat
to play soccer and
all the valentines fell out.
Everyone laughed.
Buster called him "Loverboy."
"Hey, Hot Lips," shouted Francine.
Arthur left when everyone sang,

Arthur and his girl friend sitting in a tree,
K-I-S-S-I-N-G.
First comes love, then comes marriage,
Then comes Arthur with the baby carriage.

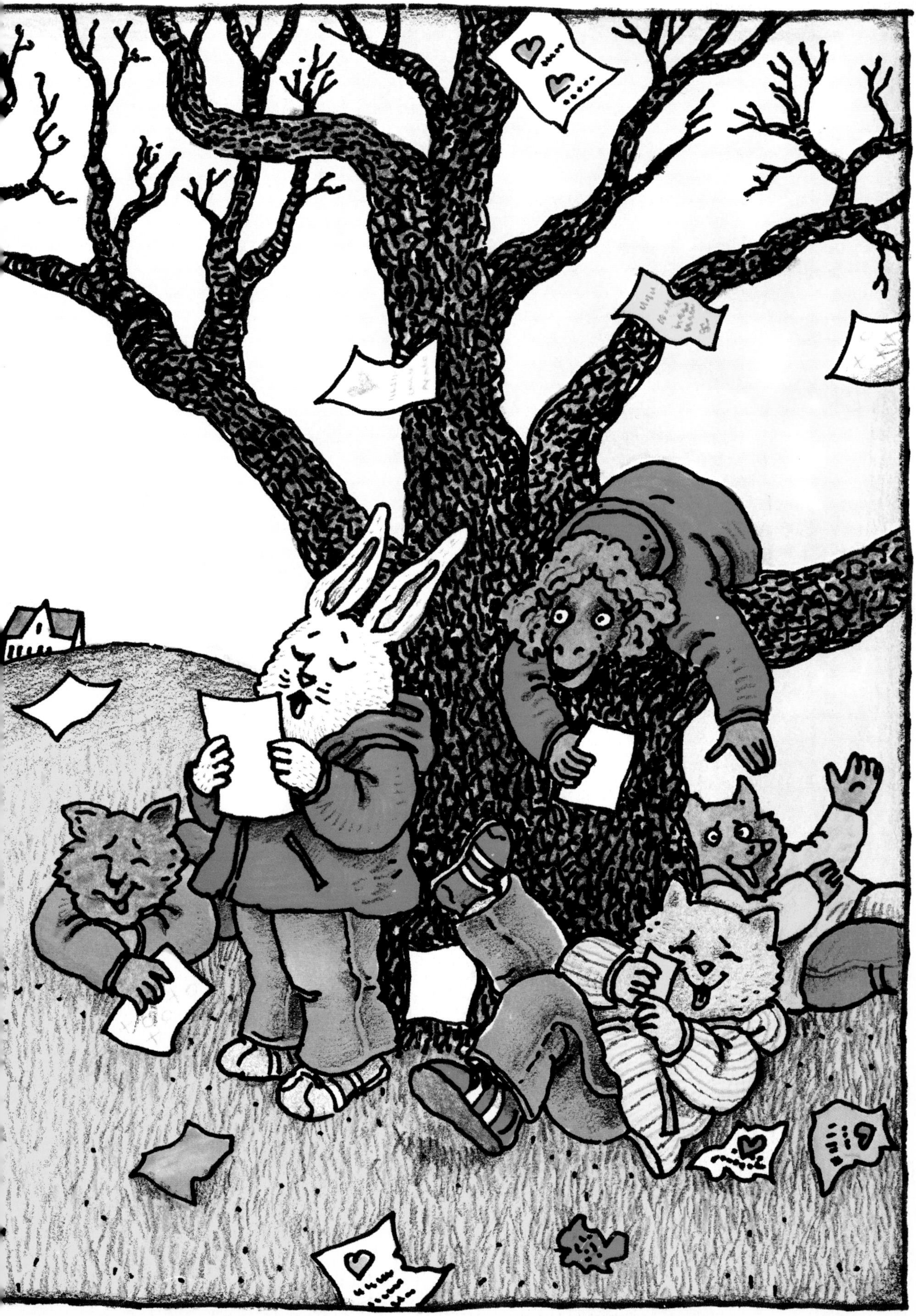

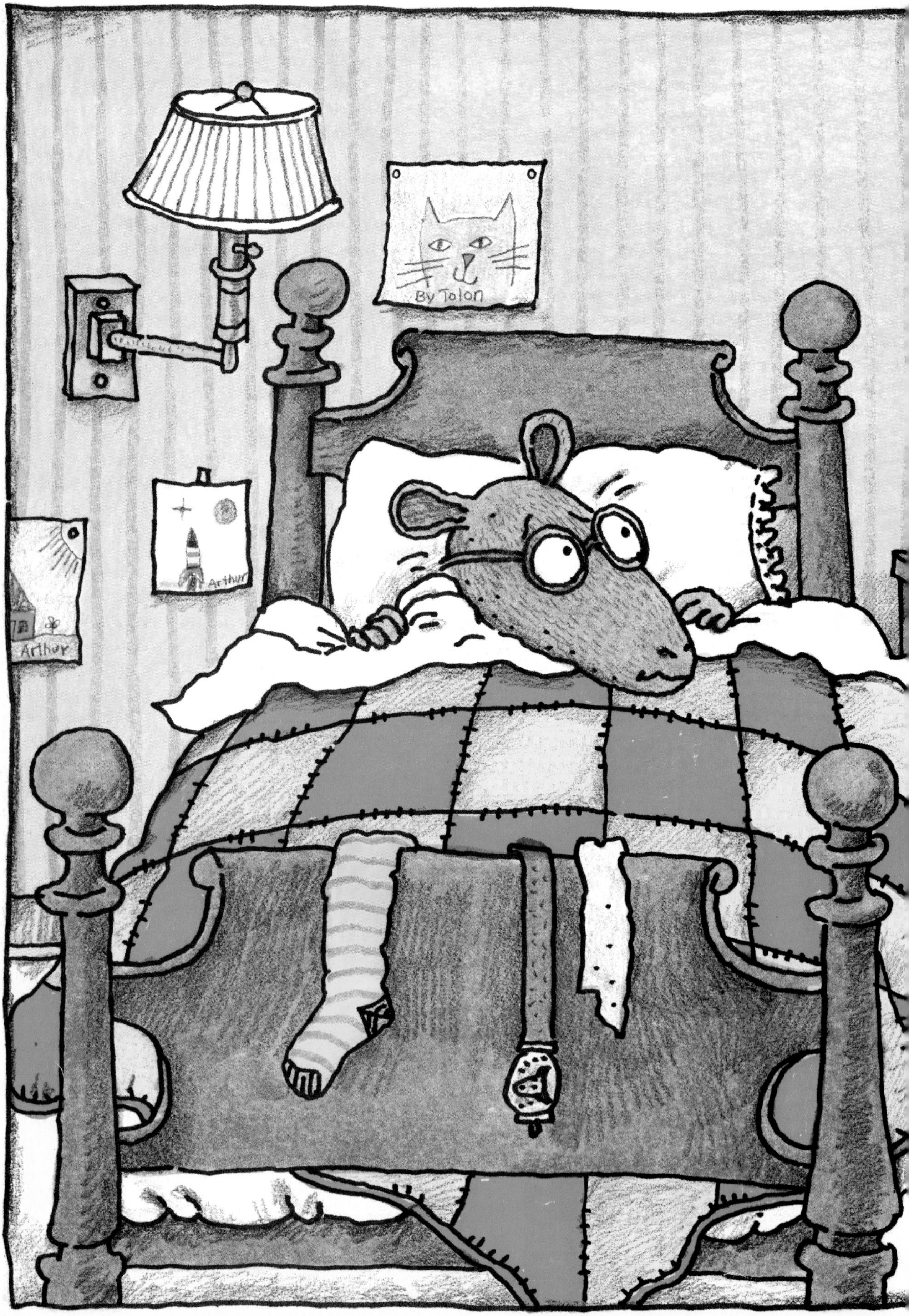
By Tolon
Arthur
Arthur

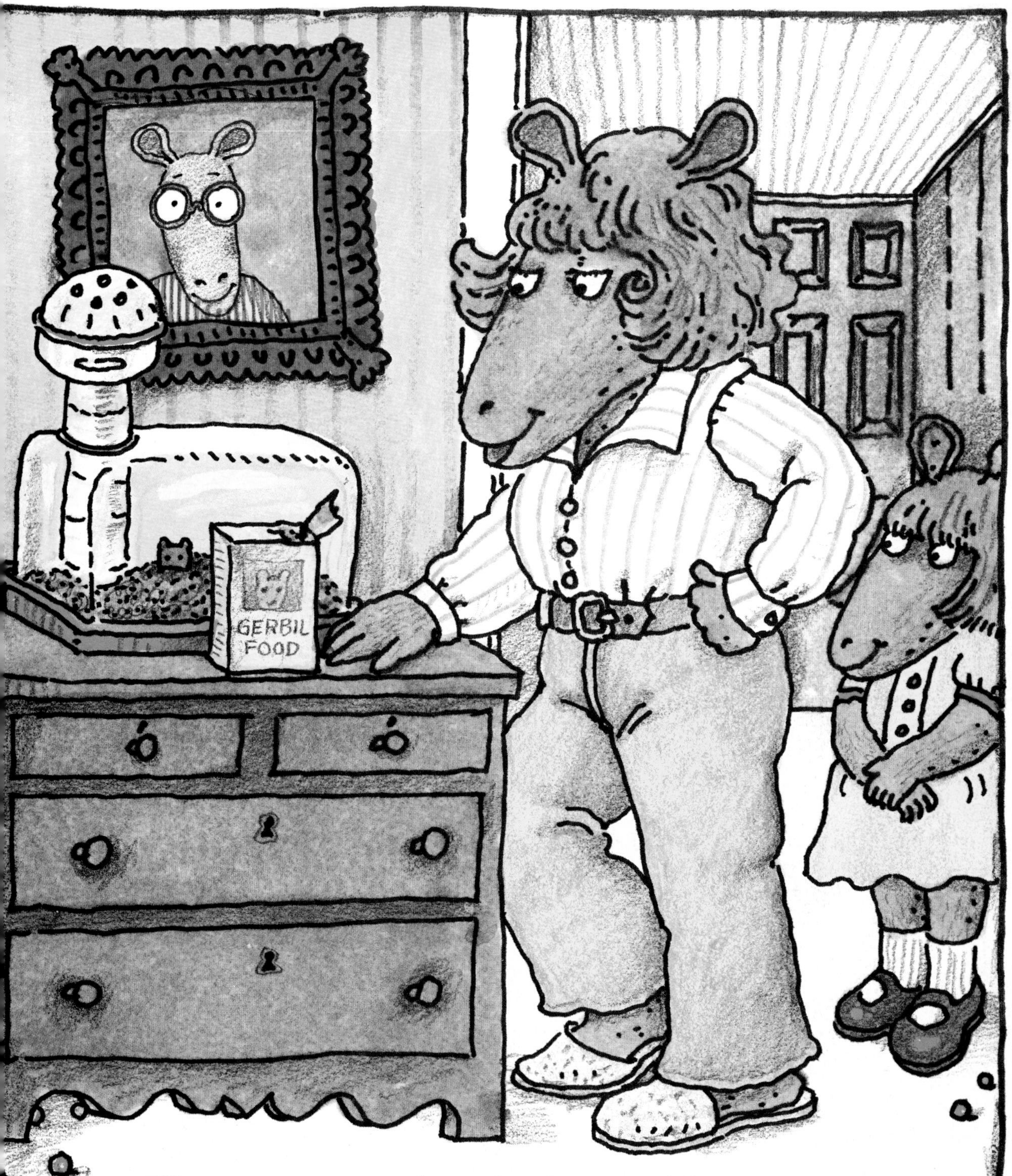
GERBIL
FOOD

**The next morning Arthur said he was sick.
"You don't want to miss
the big Valentine's Day party,
do you?" asked his mother.**

Arthur went to school.
"Ick! Who sent this mushy valentine?"
said Sue Ellen.

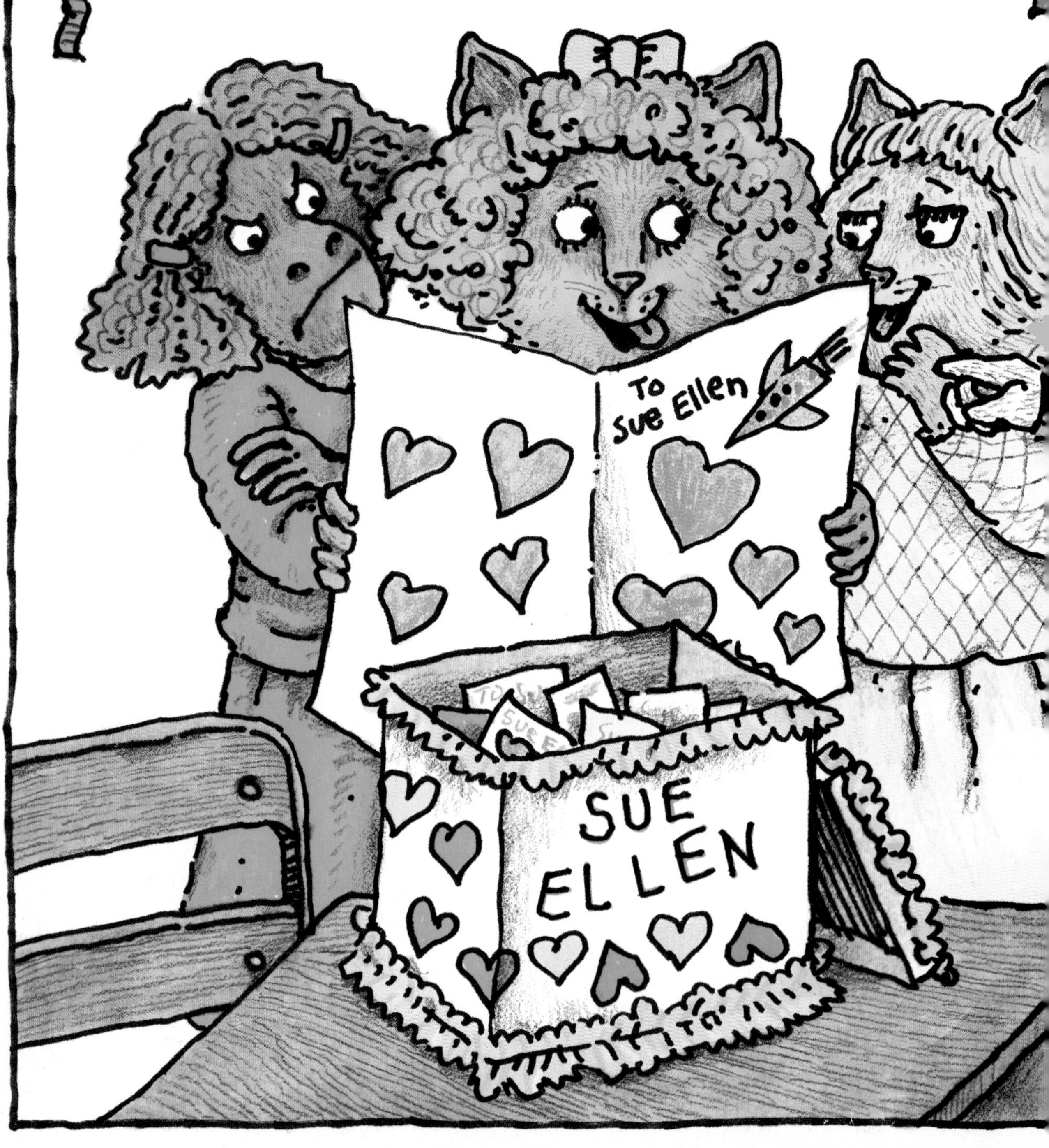
To Sue Ellen
SUE ELLEN

“It’s signed ‘Arthur,’” shouted Buster.
Everybody laughed.
“Arthur loves Sue Ellen,” everyone sang.

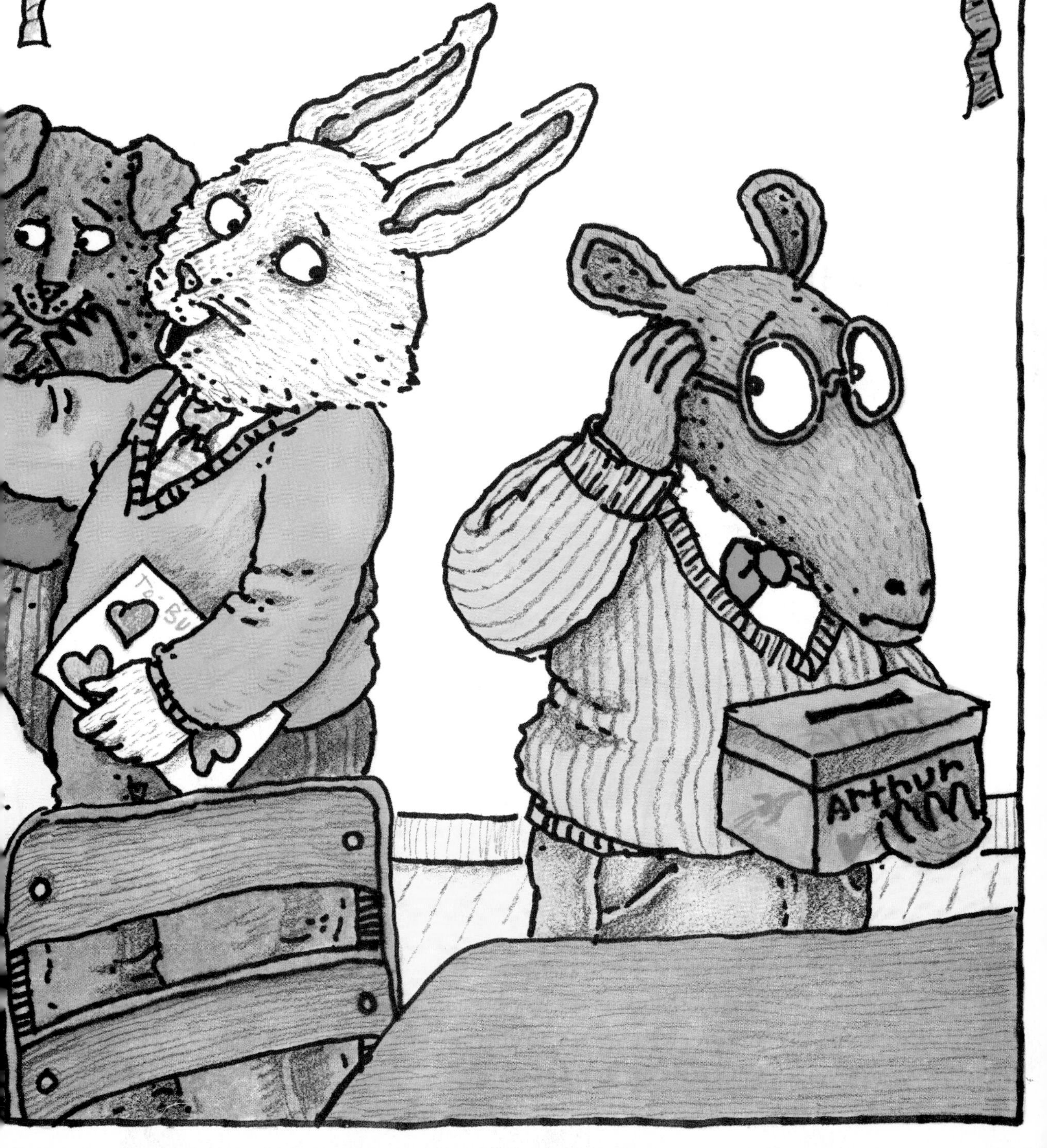
Arthur

After school, Arthur wanted to be alone.
On the way home, he climbed up
to his tree house.
There he found another valentine.

I love you in London,
I love you in Rome.
Look in your mailbox
When you get home.
XOXOXOXOXOXOXOXOXOXOX
Your Secret Admirer

"Oh, gross," said Arthur,
and ran into the house.

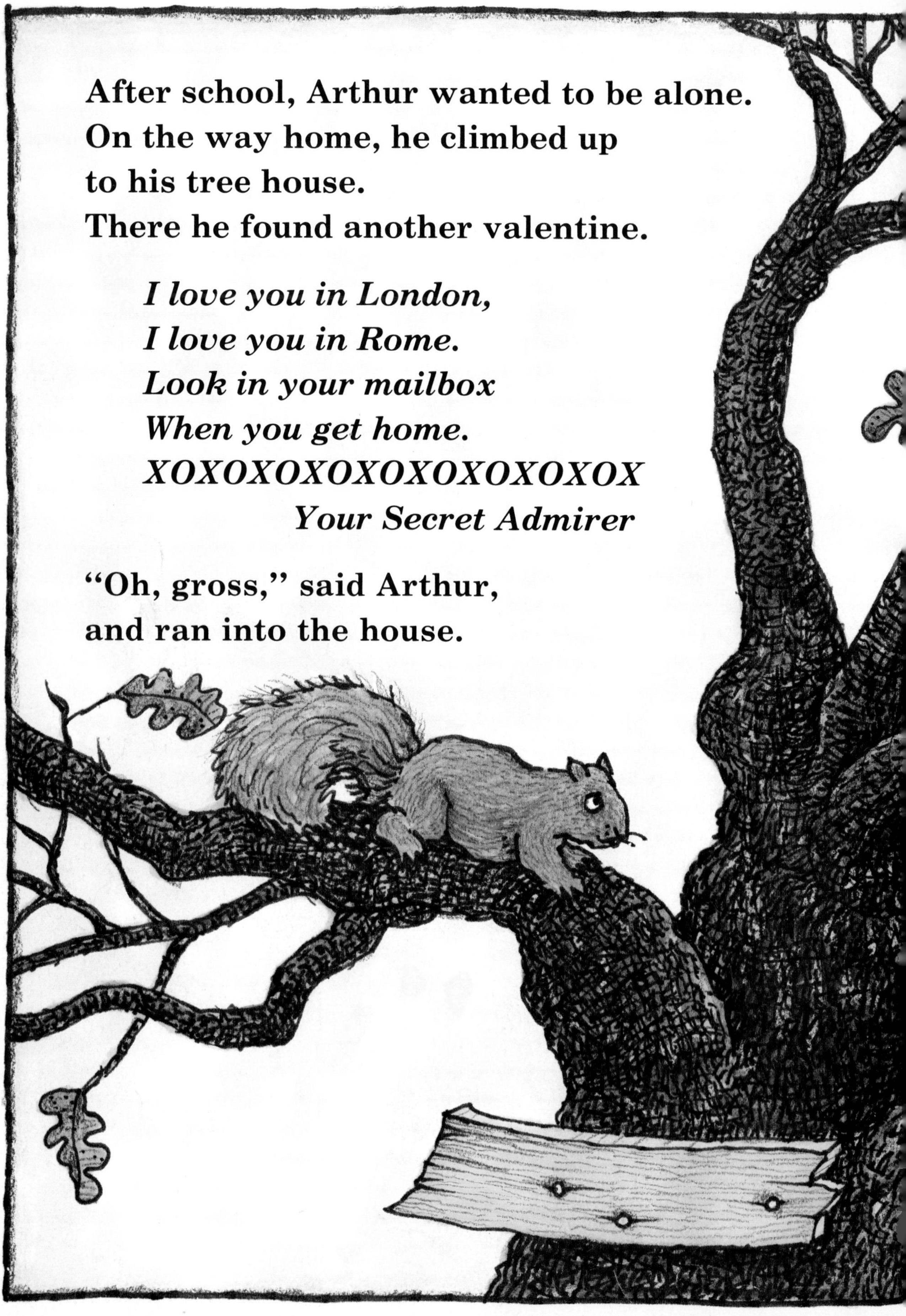

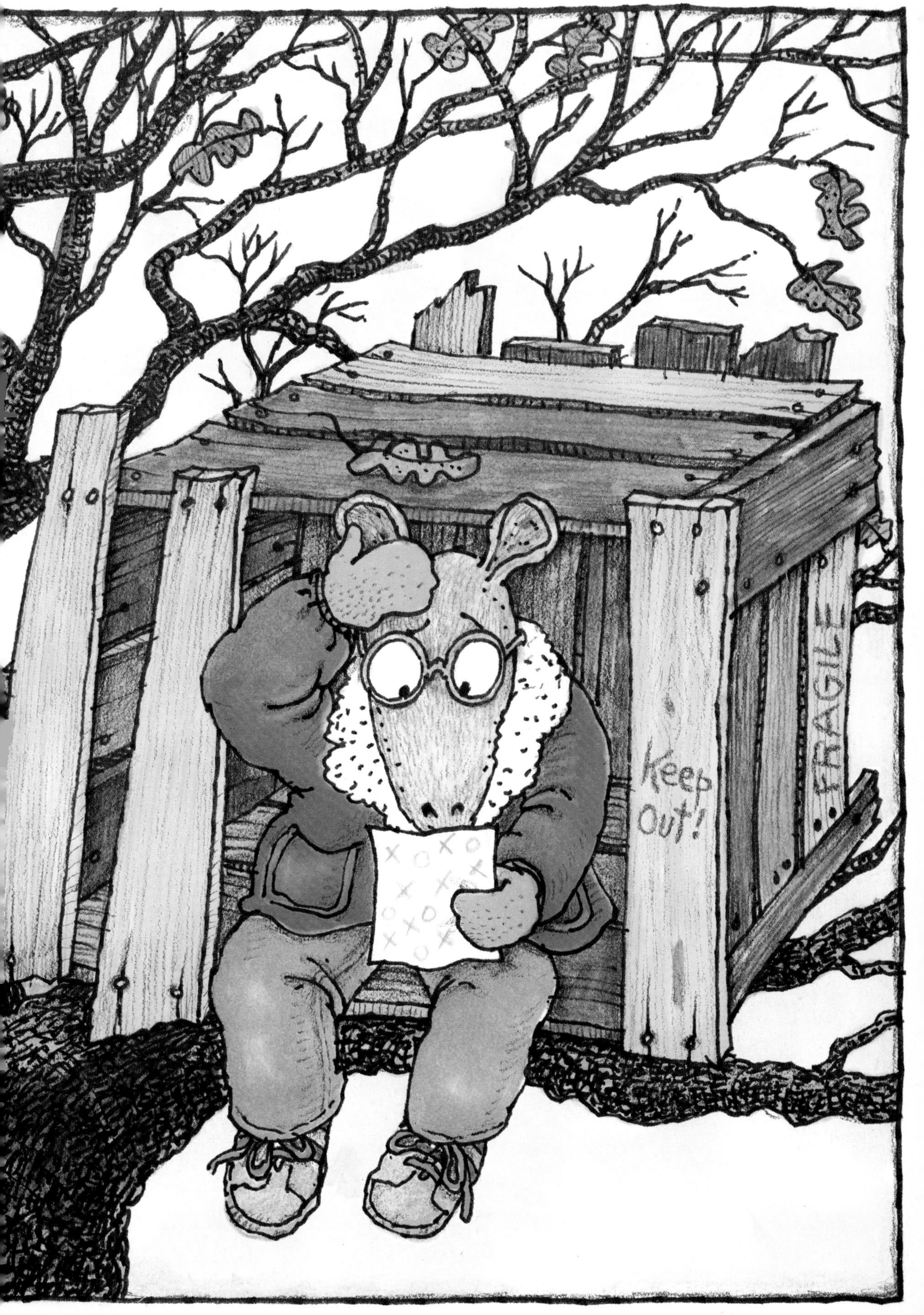
Keep out!
FRAGILE

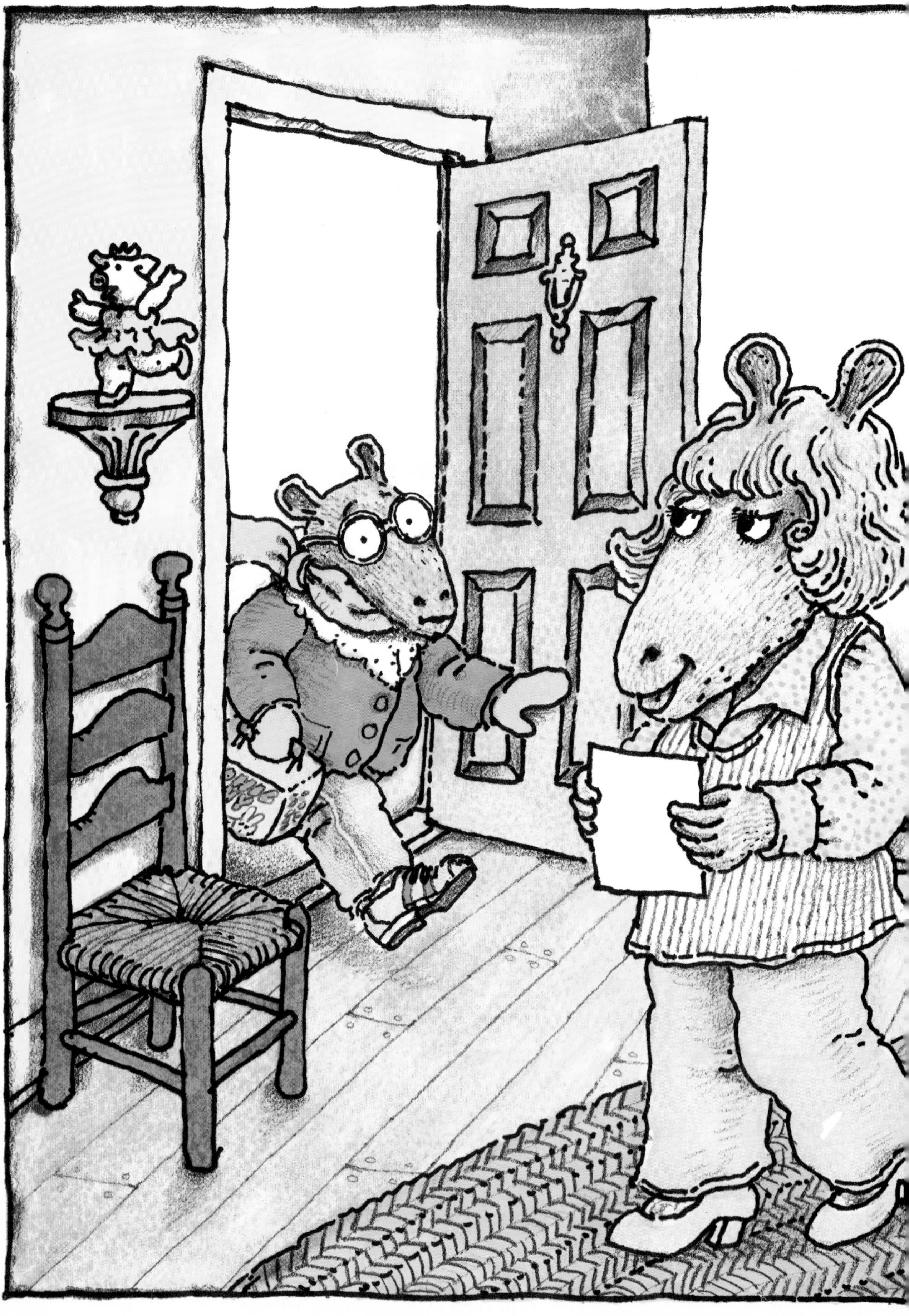

"I believe this is for you, Arthur,"
said his mother.
"It's a love letter," said his sister.

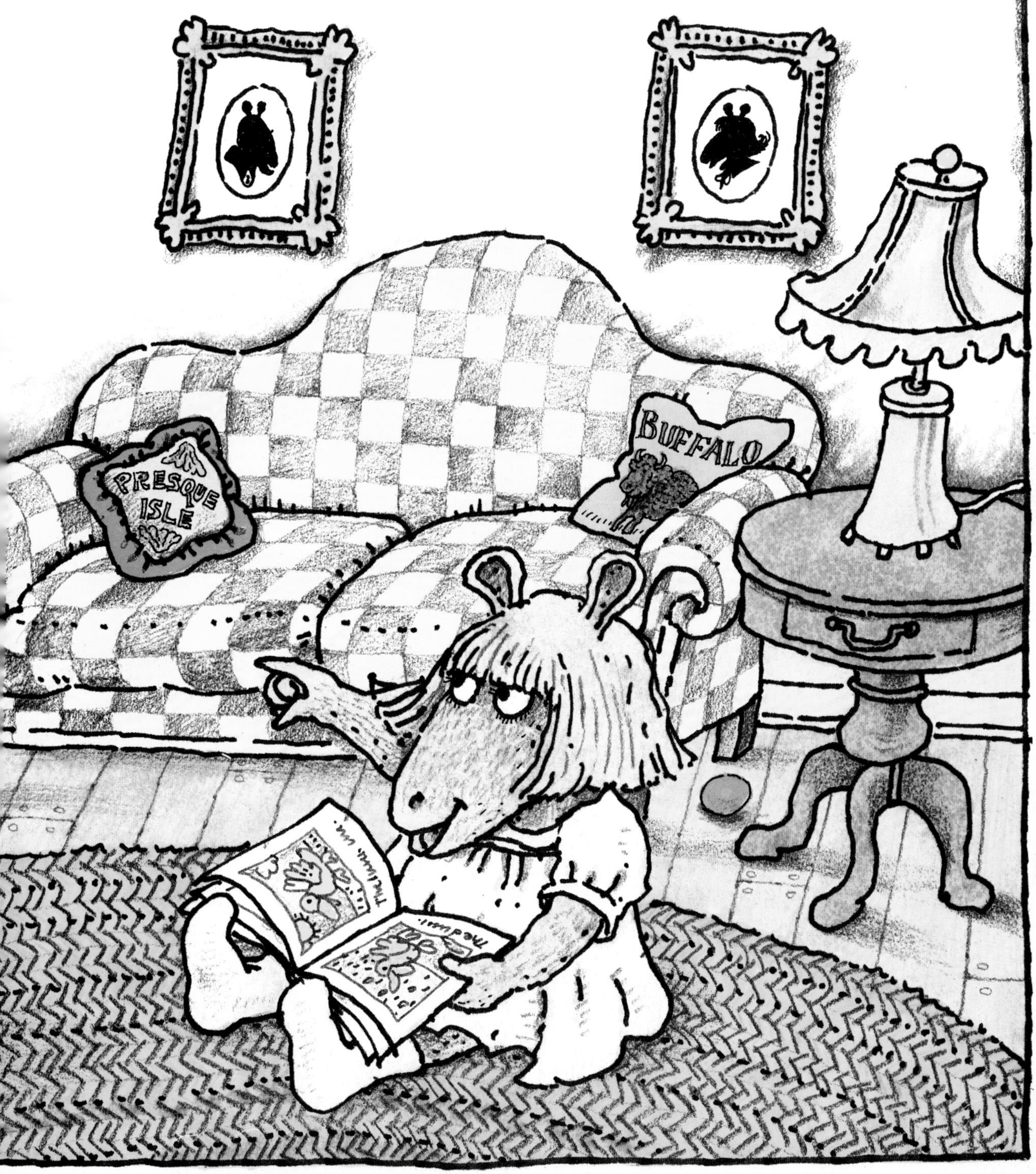
PRESQUE ISLE
BUFFALO

Arthur went to his room.
There was a movie ticket in the card.

My love, tomorrow is the day
We meet in row 3—
You in seat A,
Me in seat B.
Your Secret Admirer

On the card, Arthur saw a smudge.
He looked very closely.
Something had been erased.
There was an F and an R and an A—
F-R-A-N-C-I-N-E!

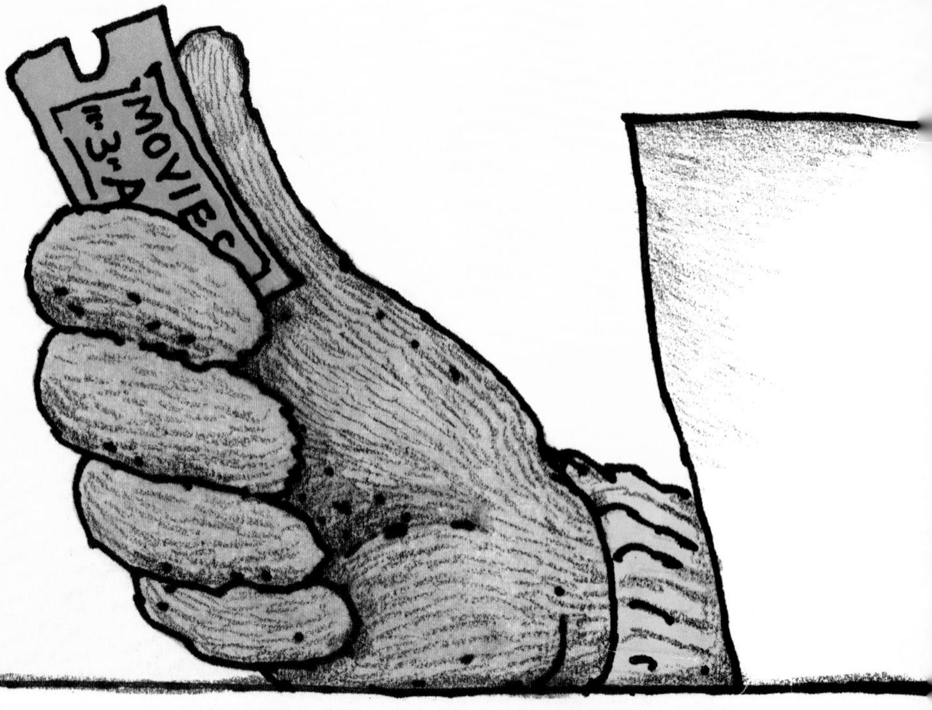
MOVIES
3rd A

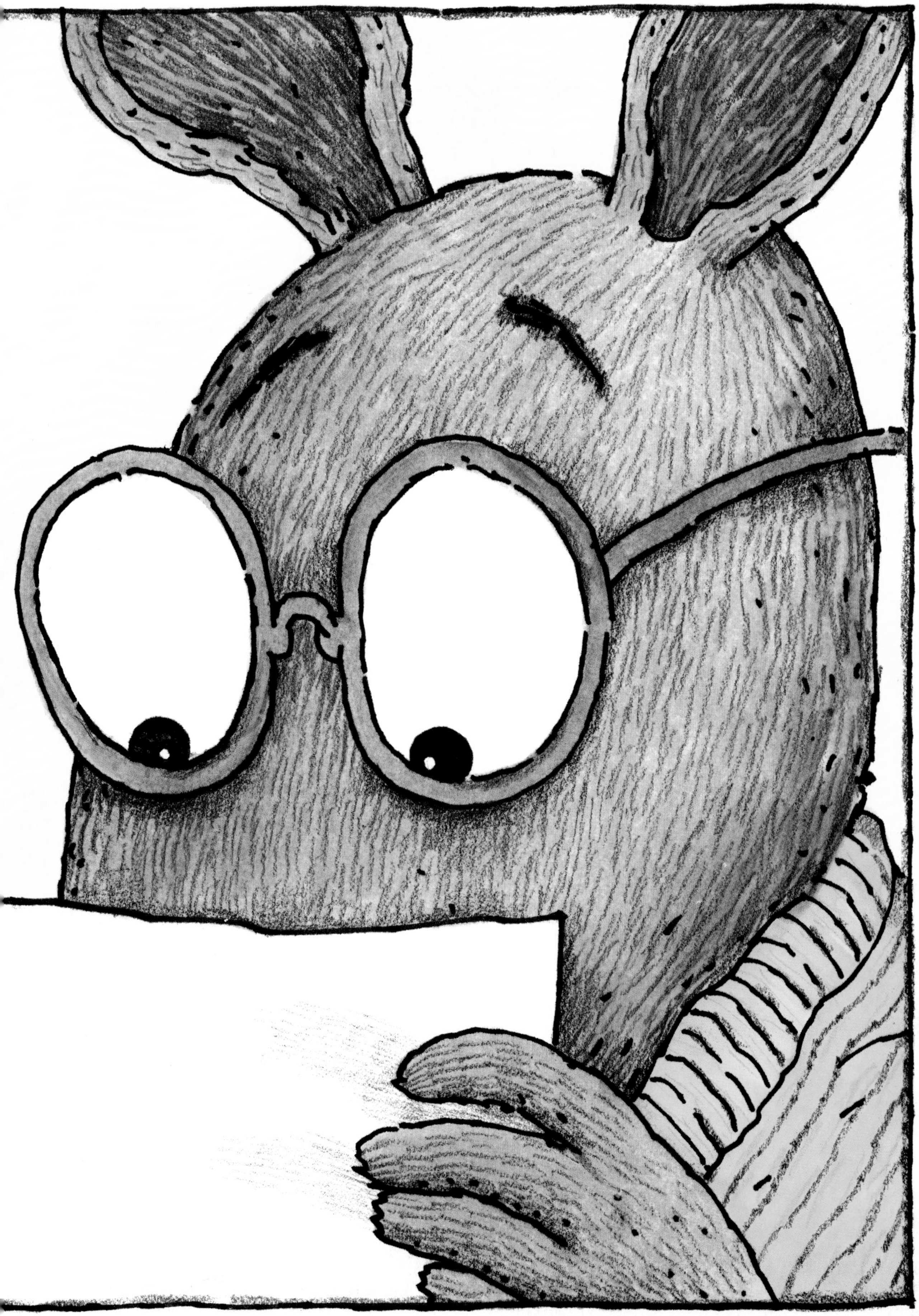

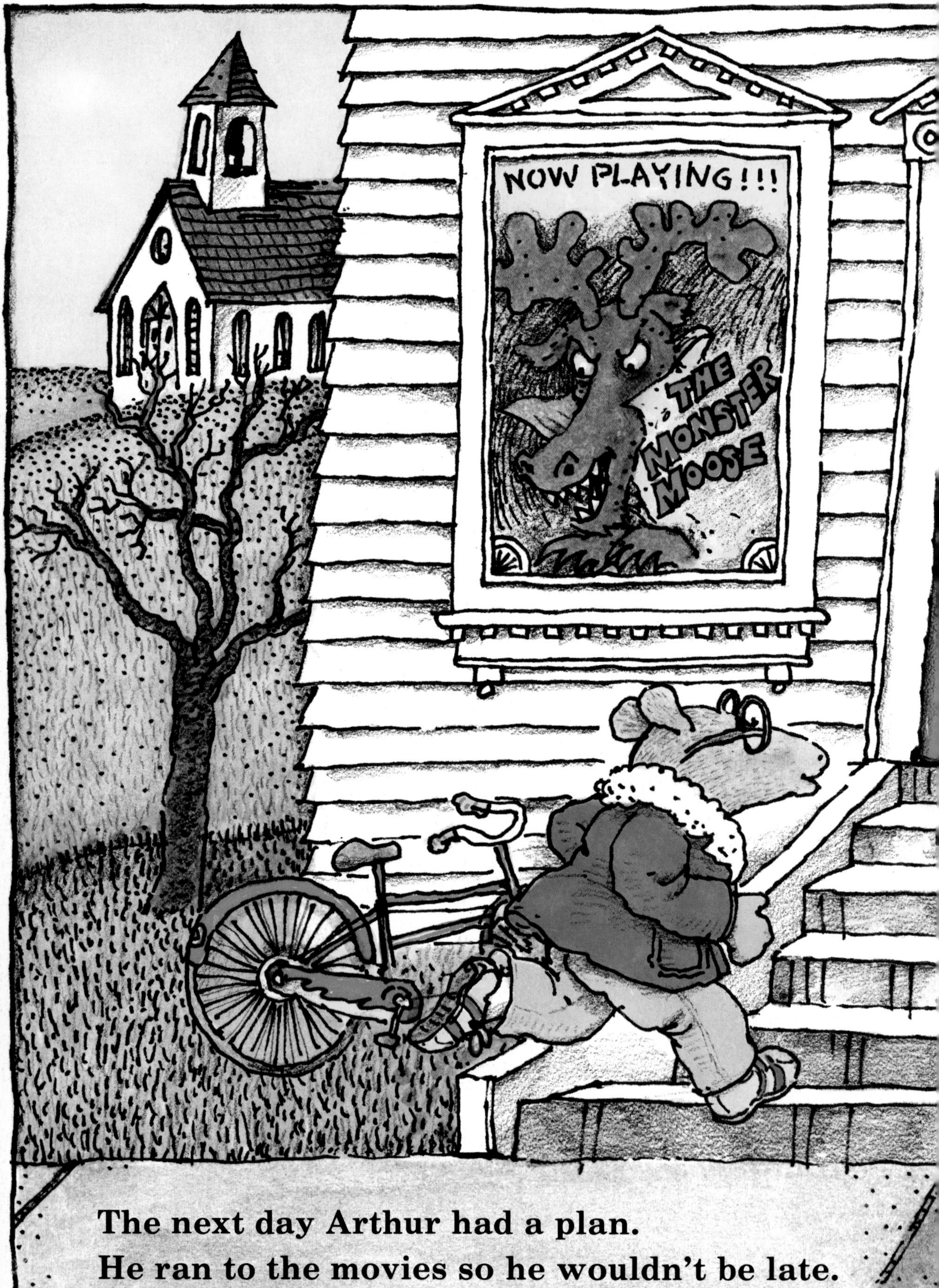
NOW PLAYING!!!
THE MONSTER MOOSE

The next day Arthur had a plan.
He ran to the movies so he wouldn't be late.

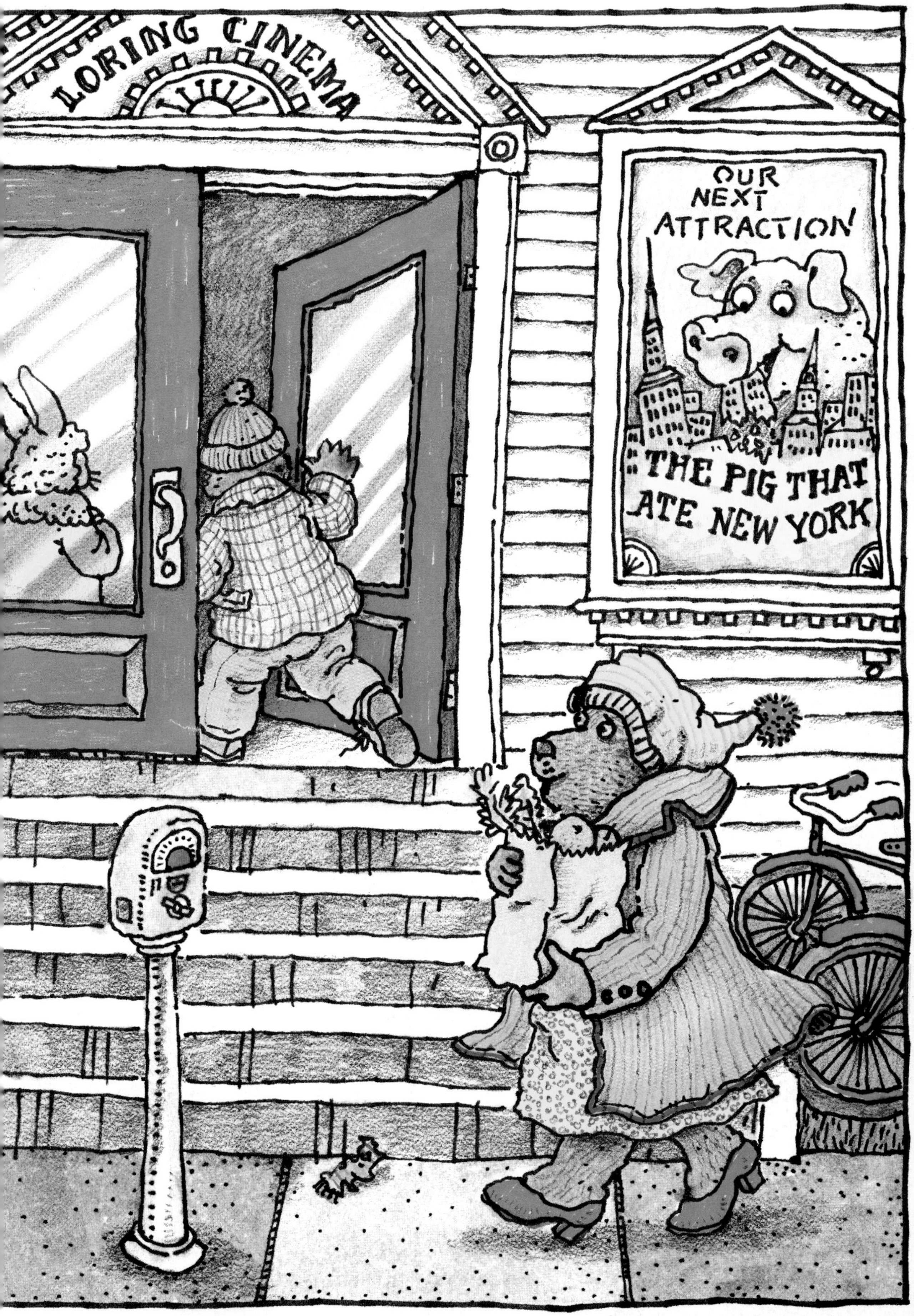
LORING CINEMA
OUR NEXT ATTRACTION
THE PIG THAT ATE NEW YORK

He found row 3.
He sat in seat A.

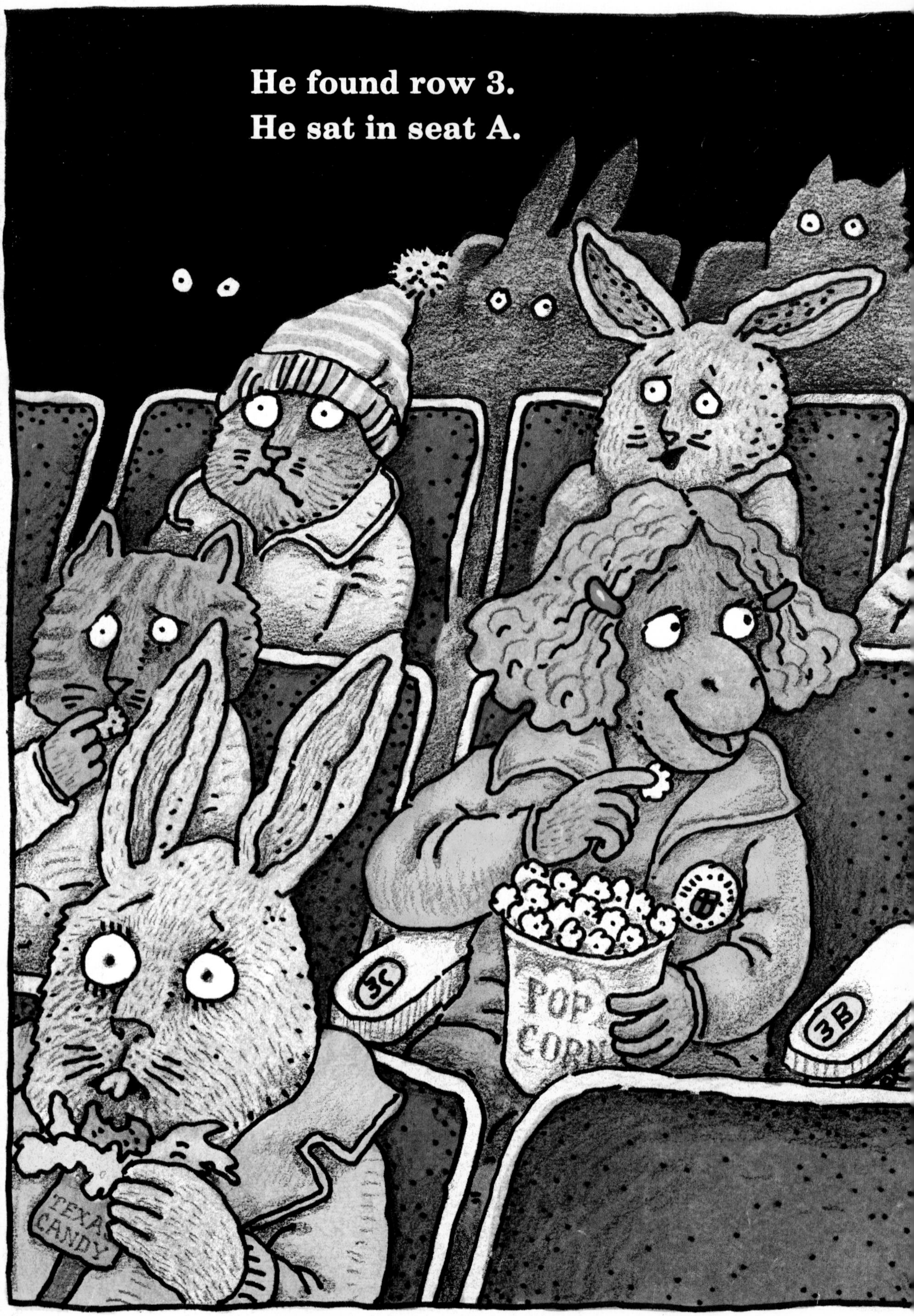
3C
POP
CORN
3B
TEXA
CANDY

Francine smiled at Arthur.
"So you're the secret admirer," said Arthur.
"Good guess, Four Eyes!"

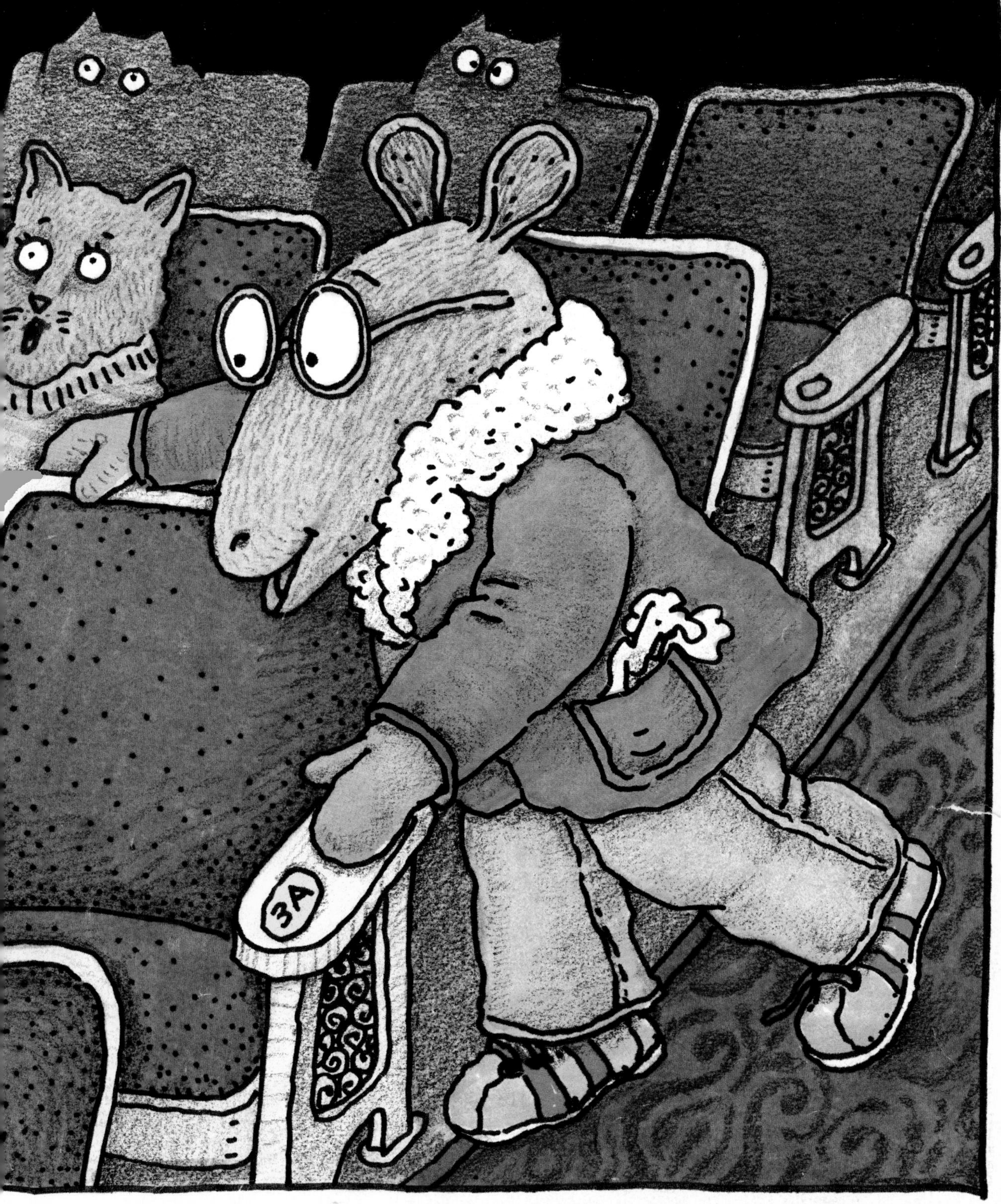
3A

"Close your eyes," said Arthur. "I want to give you a kiss."
"Really?" said Francine.
"Close your eyes and count to ten."
"Okay," said Francine.

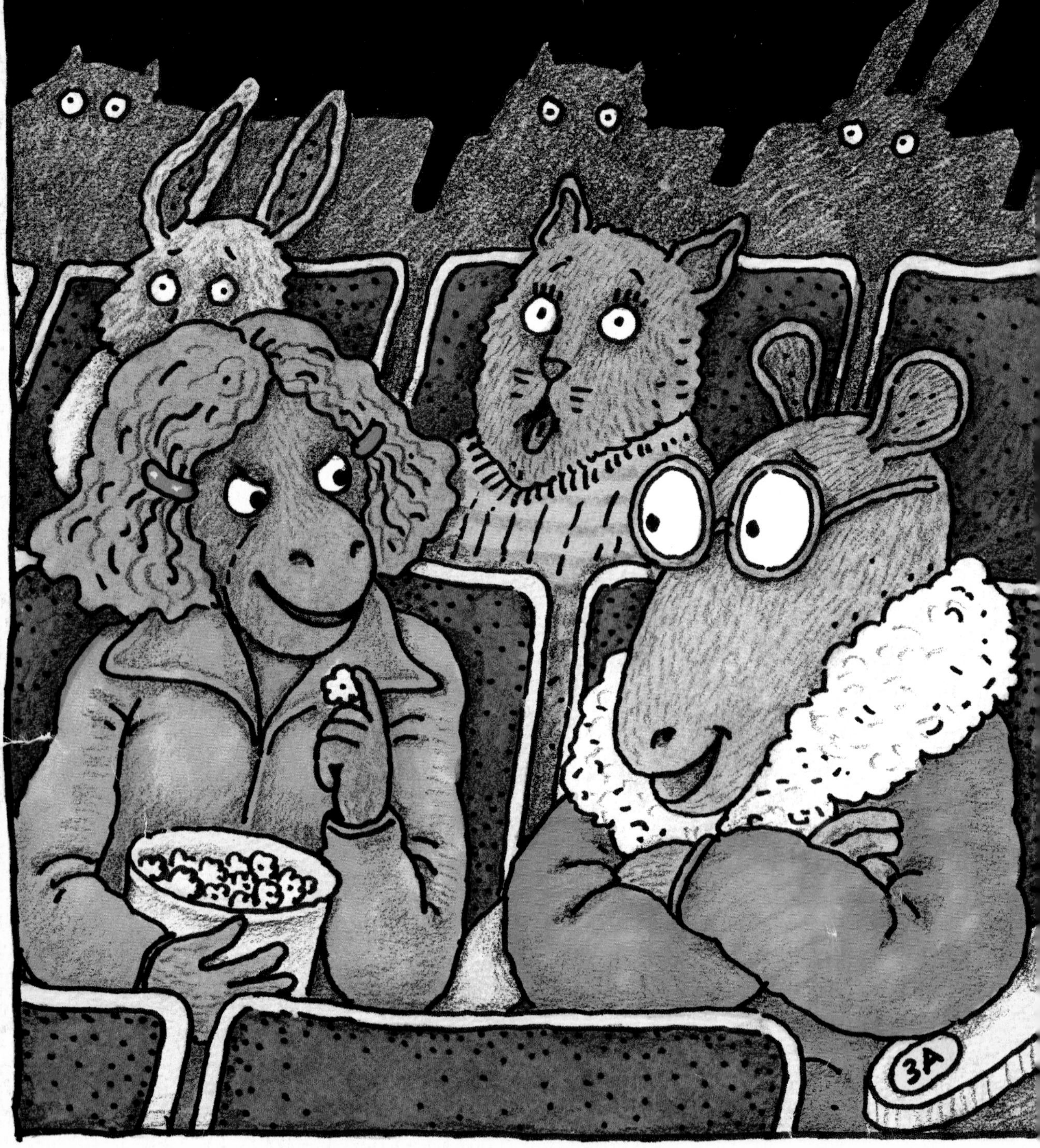
3A

"Arthur, can I open my eyes yet?" asked Francine.

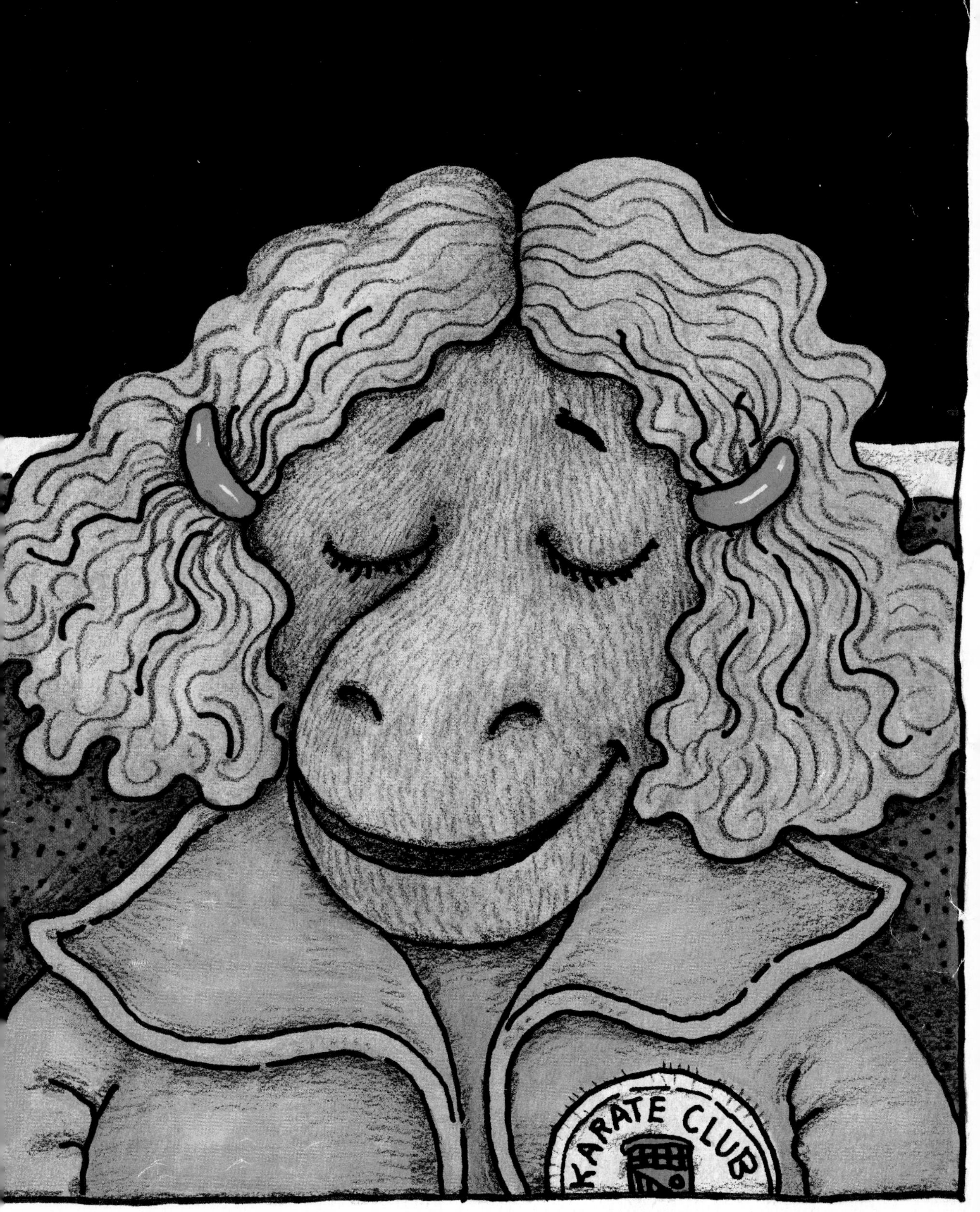
KARATE CLUB

"Arthur?"

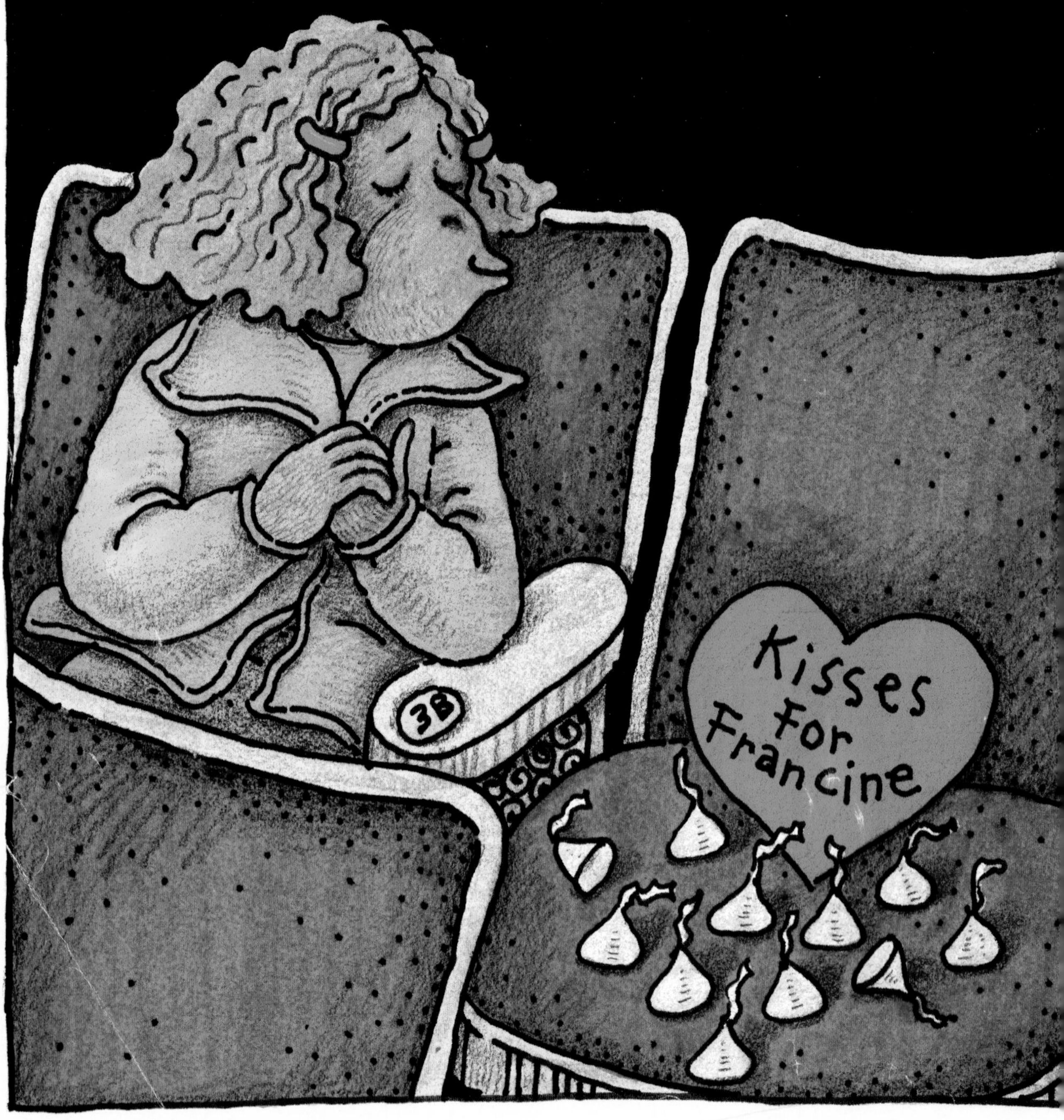
3B
Kisses
For
Francine

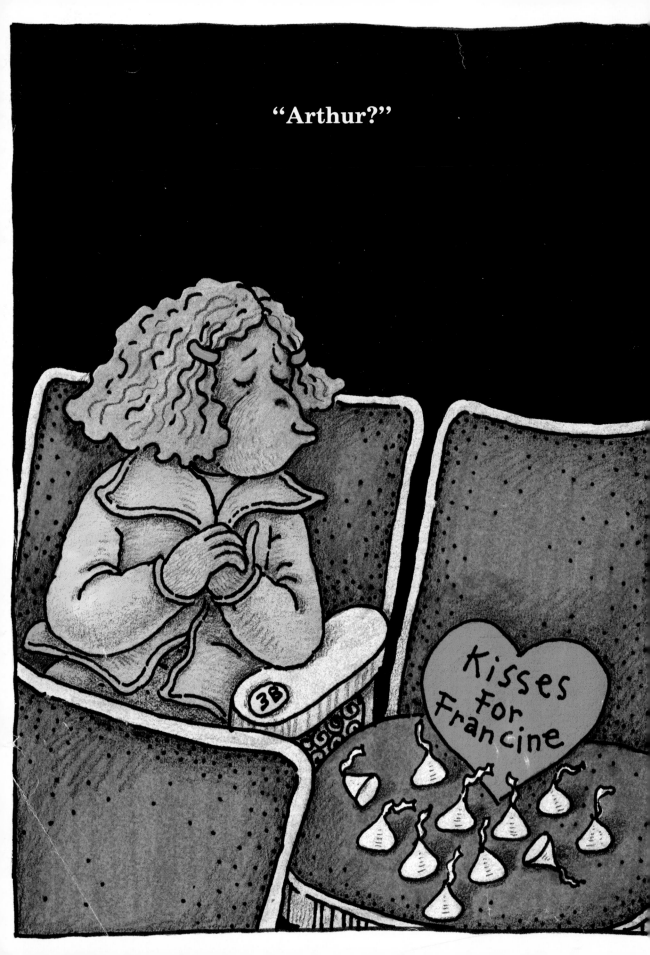

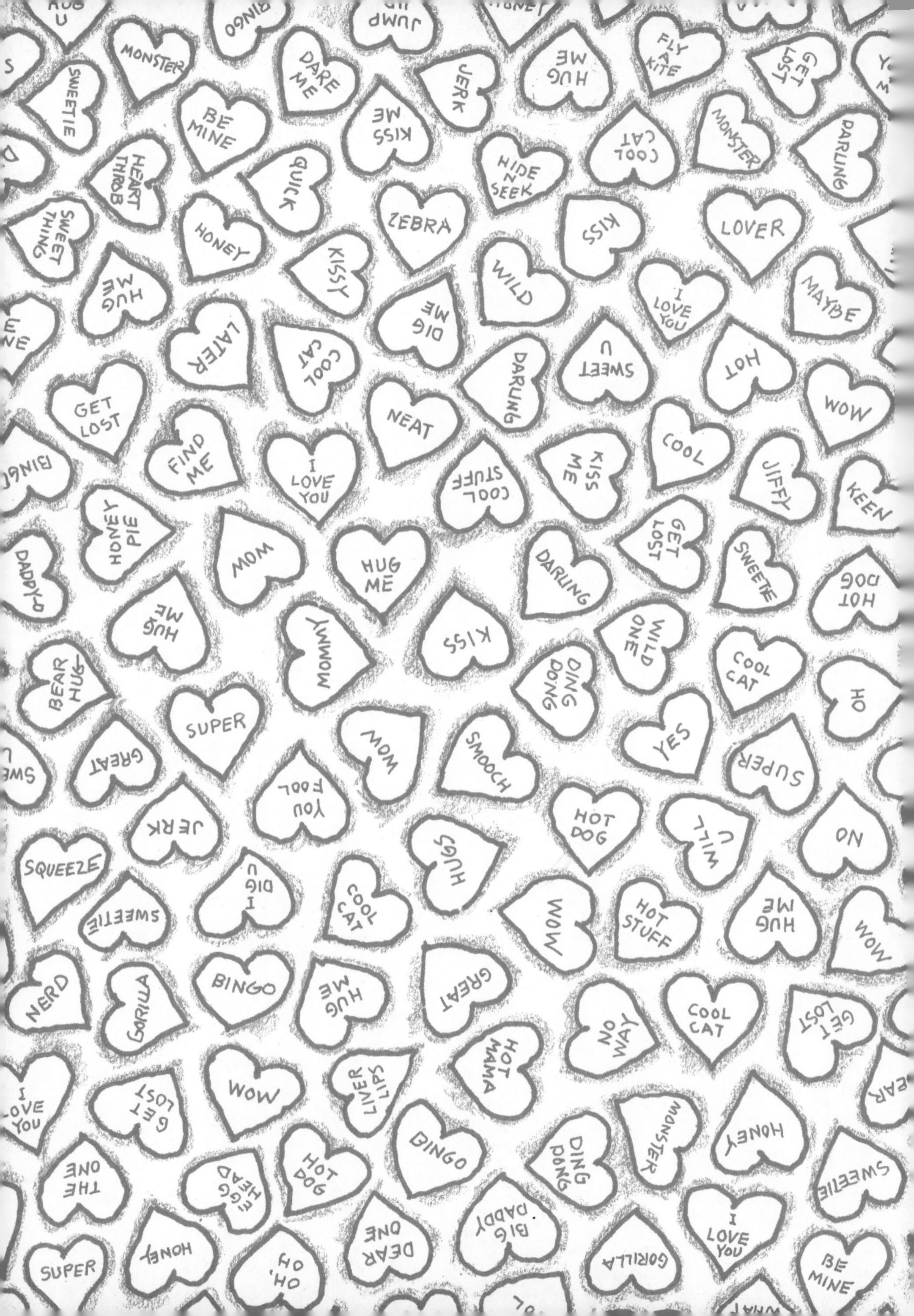
MONSTER
BINGO
JUMP
DARE ME
FLY A KITE
HUG ME
GET LOST
SWEETIE
BE MINE
KISS ME
JERK
COOL CAT
MONSTER
DARLING
HEART THROB
QUICK
HIDE N SEEK
SWEET THING
HONEY
ZEBRA
KISS
LOVER
HUG ME
KISSY
WILD
I LOVE YOU
MAYBE
DIG ME
LATER
COOL CAT
SWEET U
HOT
DARLING
GET LOST
NEAT
WOW
FIND ME
I LOVE YOU
COOL STUFF
KISS ME
COOL
JIFFY
KEEN
HONEY PIE
WOW
HUG ME
DARLING
GET LOST
SWEETIE
DADDY-O
HOT DOG
HUG ME
MOMMY
KISS
WILD ONE
BEAR HUG
DING DONG
COOL CAT
SUPER
YES
OH
GREAT
WOW
SMOOCH
SUPER
YOU FOOL
HOT DOG
WILL U
NO
JERK
SQUEEZE
I DIG U
HUGS
COOL CAT
WOW
HOT STUFF
HUG ME
WOW
SWEETIE
NERD
GORILLA
BINGO
HUG ME
GREAT
NO WAY
COOL CAT
GET LOST
HOT MAMA
I LOVE YOU
GET LOST
WOW
LIVER LIPS
MONSTER
HONEY
BINGO
DING DONG
THE ONE
EGG HEAD
HOT DOG
SWEETIE
BIG DADDY
I LOVE YOU
DEAR ONE
HONEY
OH, HO
SUPER
GORILLA
BE MINE